MW01592336

Time Impairment

by Randy Jones

RoseDog❖Books

PITTSBURGH, PENNSYLVANIA 15238

The contents of this work including, but not limited to, the accuracy of events, people, and places depicted; opinions expressed; permission to use previously published materials included; and any advice given or actions advocated are solely the responsibility of the author, who assumes all liability for said work and indemnifies the publisher against any claims stemming from publication of the work.

All Rights Reserved
Copyright © 2017 by Randy Jones

No part of this book may be reproduced or transmitted, downloaded, distributed, reverse engineered, or stored in or introduced into any information storage and retrieval system, in any form or by any means, including photocopying and recording, whether electronic or mechanical, now known or hereinafter invented without permission in writing from the publisher.

RoseDog Books
585 Alpha Drive, Suite 103
Pittsburgh, PA 15238
Visit our website at *www.rosedogbookstore.com*

ISBN: 978-1-4809-7122-6
eISBN: 978-1-4809-7099-1

Time Impairment

New York teamed to life with New Yorkers from one location to another. Movies, clothing and housing in one of the biggest cities in the world. The poster pictures and the portraits showed building that reached the sky. Civilization with differed restaurants, some with cola, and others with food, the buildings at night took on a hue with lights up to the sky. The business was a to z, expensive of inexpensive with portrait studios, bars, night clubs, movies, cars, etc. Eight hour work day workmanship brought housing paid groceries for a week and a ticket to the show or the Knicks game.

The school buses ran education and were highly rated in the New York. Steve Thomas worked through the Confederate Army to our most recent war. Wars were recreated through time or should one state documented. Women that fought over rights I do not want to get women in the class fevered on superstition Steve paused. He knew that if he gave the girls permission they would be riddled for a while. The blacks the same. If the homosexuals came forward the same antagonism. He knew to pause on certain subjects caused trouble if he heated the debate and without knowing it. The student responded easily. If the subject could be brought back with the charges of profanity and he or she that was told not to respond.

The treatment of women, blacks, gays, etc., bills were passed in the White House. If blacks could not sit at the front or the back of the bus inquire why to the bus driver. Find out how many were offended and after asking the police officer. If it were legal for black, women, and gays to be discriminated against.

If not hostile to your race, religion, sex or pestering him during the officers work day. He may tell you that blacks worked in another location that elderly black women have a hearing disability or that it was believed that blacks promoted crime in that area. After checking with the officer and finding out if the state employee was correct or not. If you find prejudice find another alternative to go that route, get signatures and the police report on individuals and support from Washington. The people violated and if it were lawful and whether or not the state such as the state police and city police back you against hostilities and verbal attacks. You can go with the police report, laws, and bills passed means the state department backs amendments with education and procedure backed by the police. If not find another route.

Steve Thomas stated that would be on the test. The test was founded in fact from the text book. Steve's output was good for the state. The maps, the military generals, the length of the way. History was recorded and Steve drew the chapters out and gave assignment and pages and instructed. His pay was enough. He answered to the president.

Present Day

The United States military went to freezer units. Cuba assaulted America upon being taken hostage, does anyone play stage 3. Stage 3 meant that you signed at the state police office and the government tests you. A computer said on two million Americans, said I and were given poison. The US assaulted us with written signatures was Cuba, Cuba rose forward and took the hostages. The military computer said on, the United States was at war with Cuba. The belonged to Cuba. One hundred percent of the United States was hostage. Cuba shouted ordered and the United States spoke none. The presidents business continued. He spoke to foreign well. His ruin was forgotten that he was dead asleep would be take advantage of by an AAA paradise baby.

Stetson was back in his pen. He knew the United States was hostage and that the military was frozen until money was processed and that Cuba was the aggressor that held America hostage. While the country was cross matched, Cuba linguistic vocal somehow spoke American. While coming into America on a four automatic character. The country looked the same yet Cuba had over taken one hundred percent through the president. Stetson knew military procedure when a double was placed in you could not tell the difference.

Steve Thomas wore down in a full day. His past was his past. His first girl-friend was frozen in the sun. His academics were high upon changing schools. An uneducated military man became his eighth grade teacher with military strategies in education. A straight military man Sidd Logan met at an army base to get Bob Yugun an uneducated private in the military though the educational system. Bob later went on to teach other grades. There were about one hundred that was sent in and some were there previously. One hundred would look around and say eighth grade like it was a military strategic move. It was an embarrassment to the educational system and was not against lack of education in the south and other regions. Other regions that had drought and had to stay home for farm work, Bob from New York seemed polished and educated. He was rude and different. He was given a wife that was taught later in life education and was to teach him to behave well with signals. His education was equal to his grade. In school it was very unusual for a seventh grade principle to get involved with a student that moved and to contact the military to intervene. Instead of letter him catch up or telling him he failed a grade. The military usually had high standards on education and the school board knew no better than to educate with discipline.

Stetson was in the president's office. He stated the death of his wife to the president. The president called for a cease fire and told the underground crew to bring them back to the United States underground. Tell them not to laugh at the president a forbidden fruit and they stay on top of the ground. There has been an injustice in the military and court martial will continue with Cuba. Cuba received one million. They came out of freezer units. The United States came back and they were given one million for not being fed appropriately. The Cubans ate fruit for two weeks. A house full of fruit and after a week was frozen and came out on a four and ate insects.

The minister looked out at the congregation, "Welcome to our Sunday Service. The way to see eternity is to be forgiven for your sins and to live a sinless life. The Bible is fulfilled by God not man. He anoints the people or has annotated peopled to fulfill his prophecies, no vice versa. He placed people in position and output they don't, "Output is important to living a sin free life. We have to go under domination our is descendants of Christ. We have to a title to list our church of course. We believe in repentance, Baptism in the Father, the Son and the Holy Spirit. The Holy Spirit descends out of Heaven to bless upon your sins being washed away. Holy Spirit descends out of Heaven to bless upon your sins being washed away. Holy Spirit descended upon Jesus for peace after being baptized.

The head pharaoh wore white. The blood they drank was cow's blood because their nutrient count was down. Baach was a rabbi of Satan and we serve Satan, his head was shaven. The calf's blood represented nutrients from Satan. "We are of Satan and we serve Satan." The crowd chanted. United States is back. They paid repentance to Satan for behaving like they could fight and could not. Cuba was mean and ate fruit then went back to freezer units. They received compensation from the United States one hundred percent at a sum of one million dollars and ate fruit in a character found. They chased larvue, the United States smiled at their pursuit of food. We frown upon it as do most Cuban Empires. Repercussion of Satan, we wash our linen and the world is the United Sates that pretended to fight and could not. The president was kinky one of his own Navy, lost a wife because she was a hostage did not cooperate.

Egypt won one hundred percent on an overtake of business. They sent their best representative to collect and collect they did. They could send a representative to collect and they would send someone with a knife or gun to go in the driveway of a con to ask if Egypt was this way or that. If they said anything bad about Egypt's politics or Satan they would assassinate quick. Over a trillion was assassinated over the word since the 1920's. They were quick and graceful and sold business quick. The Egyptians would look intimidating when coming after business. They won high especially if it had Egyptian written on it. They just knew what to say.

Stetson was in the last pew, his wife came and went. He listened to the minister. He missed her. The rain beat against the colorful plate glass church windows. He knew that military strategies were not necessarily a religion. However if you have good habits your output may be more precise. The president was not happy with his wife's death it was warfare with Cuba and she resisted a hostage situation. Stetsons prayers was to her, he thought only well of her. Stetson received an honorable discharge from the military three weeks before reenlistment. He sold the house and moved. The underground location was reentered in a micro-computer disc and filled under Stetson, retired Navy.

Stetson was happy with a new house and an output that was different. He would find a new job. The reason religion became an aspect was wars were filled under God or Satanism. As the head admiral when it was usually a disagreement in trade. The president was back and the country was back. He asked that his paradise vacation not be mentioned and it was not. There was one death the president regretted, it was Stetson's wife, when she did not comply with Cuban law and was assassinated.

"Hi, I'm Cuban Ambassador one three and five. We college." The college was high in output. Tim Albright was a Cuban born that was educated in America. He was fluent in both languages. His output was high. His friend from Cuba was two million. He had equity from the state department of two million. He followed Cuba none because they ate insects. He was gifted at math and showed it by aggravating no one but teachers at precise. He learned the language at three. He was an elite family son at five because he applied American customs well to his Cuban heritage. He had an IQ of one ninety. The highest of intelligence quota being two hundred. He showed his IQ by being Hispanic instead of Cuban he gained. He went to school eight hours a day just like a job. He succeeded because he was very much output in the right areas. Upon reviewing the case of Stetson he would have stated he was wrong. He should have taken the military and killed Cuba. Stetson hated his wife's death yet it was settled by the president. If he looked Al Capone's record up from a neutral perspective he would state he was right because the state department came in on Capone. He did not go in on them. He was an ace at figuring situations out and filling them forever. He looked at them again none. He went to school every day of his life after sixteen for twenty years. He was in freezer units from Cuba and came out at thirty eight. The Cuban Ambassador was generous at freezing him to learn the American life.

His IQ was high from birth. His job from Cuba or work assignment was your Cuban stay Cuban. The war that was started by President Byer's, Tim Albright Cuban and his built the organization to one trillion one thousand times. The time of Tim's education had to be trillions of years ago. IT was a very long time ago, billions trillions of time, perhaps his organization was established a very long time ago. President Byers did not know his race. He wore rabbi of the Middle East and was the same as a Devil from Hell. He succeeded in billions. His estates were trillions. He stated Egypt the head pharaohs head was shaven. He was an original Egyptian. President Byers contact the head pharaohs. The United States had meditation. You clear your head and though process is that you wanted to have output in, sometimes music was activated. A suggestion was the sea, the jungle birds, lightning storms, sometimes music was activated. A suggestion was the sea, the jungle birds, lightening storms, sometimes treatment that was state meant the US approved that it fell under guidelines of the state and was safe. If not protocol would instruct the counselors that were paid for by the state and was safe. If not protocol would instruct the counsel on how to behave legally without hostility towards situations. In their lives the instructions was a balance back to normal if the family attended group and ask questions. They would know of the changes if they did not process well. They could see a doctor on individual bases and try to think and act better. The mediation involved religion no more than it was the same before.

The Egyptians were very keen rabbis or priest. Their education was high. Their temples dark, their mediations to the Devil. Egypt, "How do you feel about the US being taken hostage?" "I agree that they are arrogant at warfare." His head was shaven. The Egyptian were older than time it. Some would say a baby could take him. He would smile and say very much I like babies with a smile. Don't you. The militaries of the Middle East were tough and very well trained. They knew no better. The countries such as Egypt that spoke English knew how to speak well. We bought product and America generated it well. We paid one hundred percent. They delivered one hundred percent. The pharaoh was Tim Albright. He was an original Egyptian that was Cuban.

"Okay, drug deals go today Mr. Capone?" John Gotti wore a suite worth five hundred dollars. He ate breakfast, lunch and dinner at the Hyatt. His favorite food was egg benedict. John was trained for the Sicilian Mafia at age ten. The year was 1930. He was abducted by the police at eleven. The officer, Officer Mallone of the Chicago Police Department pointed, "You're under arrest." He stated. "Are you one of the rodents Capone's?" The officer's name was John Mallary. He was paid one penny. He said, "That's all." He would work for the state department for free. He police training was two years of college. His law enforcement. The year was 1930 equal to present day. He was a good officer of the law. His IQ was one eighty, he studies in school high. He took the one penny and paid rent. It paid for one year. It should have cost three pennies for one year. The land owner thought that he should get perks. He got the same officer Malone scrooge food off the neighbors. He told the neighbors that he ran out of food this week. They provided their chances of arrest were the same.

Al Capone was acquitted of tax invasion ten years earlier . In the Chicago Tribune it said Al Capone Acquitted. It showed Al with a big check that had one million on the bottom. It said black market. "Are you a rotten no good Capone?" Officer Mallone asked the ten year old John Gotti, Al's youngest brother. "No sir." Gotti responded. "You are under arrest for evading an officer." Officer Mallone stated. John presented a .38 and fired. He ran. "A body Al. He was after me because I was a Capone." John ran New York under the administration of Al and the Sicilian Mafia. He had one trillion soldiers. Al Capone said, "Deals are on. Ask Andersons if I have a ruin today." Jim Davison said, "No we apologize that we were not respectful." "Drug deals are on." Al stated.

The call went straight into Stetson's office. "Drug deals are on for the Sicilian Mafia." The caller was Conan O'Brien. "First please don't call me." Stetson said. "The mafia was cleared of all charges. Al Capone was clear of tax invasion in a United States court system in the year 1920 to 1930's and he was reissued spendable money." Stetson responded. "Come one, we can get him can't we. He's running drugs right into the veins of the United States. I was to run him through competitive systems because he's the biggest and he's running drugs." Conan wore a suite and tie. "No he would have to be incarcerated by a judge and handed over to us through the state police after being completely broken down. Did someone convince you that a family member of yours was killed by crime?" Stetson asked. Conan frowned. "Yes, I figured it out. It was a lie." "What are you in, announcing games?" Stetson inquired. "Because the pay is good and I get known." "Al is free of charges. Thanks." Conan hung ups.

Drug deal went annual and made the mafia one trillion. The Sicilian Mafia was very smart organization and showed crime none. The ocean came in with a green moss for one mile. It was a progressive food. The exotic location was fed by waterfalls, springs and rainwater. The ocean came and went when it wanted. It took and killed in seconds. Some though that is was exotic, even pretty. It killed in seconds and flooded for miles. The proofs was any last flood. The ocean was documented. This location had spiders as big as a human. They hung from webs and ate any meat; goat, wild boar. They become their last victim. In human form only a second if there were no humans around or years if they were around humans. They would kill anything alive. Political meant they went on, the opposition did not. The only other spider was the Fiddler. These human sized black widow males were one that the females died when they checked on a flood and drowned. They looked like cave women. They had characters because they did not want to be detected by the men of male spiders. The males hung down to the ground in webs and didn't move. There were trillions of them. The exotic location was lush and green and went on one trillion miles. The oxidation to the United States sixty eight percent to percent during the winter. It was the Brazilian Rain Forest. Nobody ever really made it there. It was a trillion miles distant. The ocean somehow carried the breath able air to the United States.

The Bermuda Triangle was an exotic oxidation area trillions then time in the distance. No place ever flew there because of the distance. It contained a to z one trillion varieties of venomous snakes and one million spiders. The oxidation was high, one hundred percent. The United States was seventeen percent because these trees presented more oxidation. Africa was trillions of miles inhabited with one trillion one trillion snakes that were venomous and millions of spiders. Civilization set up in Africa by cobras that played Hells Angels in America. They made it. The tribes dealt drugs and the drugs somehow made it to America. The cobras were one trillion male serpents sent to Hell and they were back. They were evil. For example they would have a picture in the paper of a rattlesnake killed. The snake would be alive one hundred percent of the time, twenty six percent of the time they would be the man holding up the presumed dead snake, the snake would live his life out.

"Hi, it's Staphodor." "HI, how are you?" Are you a Cuban setting?" "No, we are Hispanic bound." The professor said. "Do you accept Cubans in this country?" "We do if you have passport and currency for a phone service." The professor of Langley Institute of Learning said, "I want to be an American citizen. How do I do it?" "You apply at the headquarters of imports and exports of the Soviet Cosmo Science of Space." "Hey aren't you Hispanic?" The professor asked. "No I am Cuban. I serve communism in no form. May I stay in your class and learn college curriculum and pass my bar exam in a Hispanic way?" "Yes, if you are legal. Let me see your papers." The professor said. "Okay I will run home and get them." He behaved like a charming Hispanic. There were one trillion Cuban makes and at least that many women. They came from Cuba and the Middle East. Early in time their education was equal to the United States early. He checked into school. The kids were trillions. The men were high or the boys, the girls were very pretty. "Hi. I'm Cuban. Can I eat here?" "Yes, Cubans are welcome. Come on come all." They are educated the same and can eat and the Cubans ate their output.

Crime was on hundred percent. Their leader IQ was on eighty. Their money would have been one trillion one billion times. They knifed people and killed them and shot them full of voodoo by pretense if you disagreed. Their deaths in enemy were one trillion. Their leader Satan like them because they actually killed Jed Clampit. The Confederacy said, "Wait a minute. Why kill them why not just tell theme your Egyptian?" "Because we collect on Egypt and get rich." "Collect away." Satan said.

Jeff Black was a dealer of drugs beyond any harvest of Columbia or of the south. The Asian etc. was local and carried addiction. The cocaine lasted about two hours. It was high in content. America like or hated drugs. Either way they were illegal and not everyone knew how much time in jail or fines the drugs carried or how they would affect your system on withdrawal. Jeff was edited into some type of text that was compatible to equal his drug dealing skills as a state department official with cunning output or wilder beast that inhabited the wild. What Stetson didn't catch was that when he arrest Jeff he copied his system down to his brother Steve and Beck suspected that their dad Dirty Harry Callahan was placed in freezer units along with the death pool secretaries. He was supposed to have killed they were AAA good looking they were born or lived. Usually after crime courses that took a couple of years they stayed in the district in which they lived. They were educated in the United States in law enforcement. They were spies seldom outside the FBI that went where the president sent them. Local law usually said that we can handle the situation.

Joe Kennedy spoke into the microphone. "We have old in America. In the state department." He wasn't wearing his glasses or hat and was very good looking. He knew better none, his glassed had steamed and he took them off. The sign read no hats. Don't think that our country is broke it is powerful. Unions are everywhere and produce results high. Don't give to the Capone's or they will rot your brain with intrigue. Al age twenty three said, "Don't talk about me please. I went to school with John. He was a friend of mine." John F. Kennedy sat two seats back from Al. They got along well. Al was ten. He spoke to John two million time. The last time the two spoke Al was twelve. He had an A average. "Don't talk to me, speak to him." Joe smiled wondering if the fog had cleared off his glasses. He wanted them so he could see well. Joe waved sideways and said off. He was after Al on stage none. Al left He pointed, "Don't stage me and I won't stage you." Al's mom showed up after the even the told Joe, "You can speak about me if you want to and Al because I'm his mother. Al signed for the untouchables two years later. It was new when it was made, it was real life documents." In crime Al won because he was prudent with tax invasion. Al was the only movie that was new, the rest were edited through year by year. How it showed Al won was all the papers read on tax invasion. They were out and they did not return ever.

"The Cuban administration, head of Cuba name…" He slurred, "Time Albright." He spoke English fluently. The reason he slurred was because his real name was the number one thousand, they numbered Cubans instead of naming them that year. John F. Kennedy's mistake was warfare. Under stage 3 with Cuba he did not wave sideways with the Cuban administration. Cuba came over in boats, they knew the English Channel and rode ferry's to Levanport, to Myers to France and to the United States. They paddled through the English Channel into America and flew from Chicago to Washington. "Is there anything on in America?" Tim asked. "Stage is on for Cuba." He said, "There were hundred at the press conference. For the military, the FBI warfare was an under stage 3. Cuba signature said one thousand stage on" "Tim one thousand waved sideways." "Stage off for Cuba." Tim stated after the wave for us. "Mr. Kennedy on for John." John said he thought that the US military would stop the Cubans from entering the country. Ten of the Cuban administration was in the White House or around John in plain clothes. The gaurds didn't frisk them for weapons. The thought that they were happy go luck Hispanics and they were the Cuban military. "So is stage on or off for Cuba?" The plain clothed Cubab military asked. He looked, "He's panicked." "On." Said John F. Kennedy. The president of the United States said. "Are you sure that you don't want to wave sir?" The Cuban has dark eyes, he looked venomous. "On." John F. Kennedy said. He smiled. "Dallas awaits, we will be there with guns." The Cuban said to his administration. John bowed, "Cuba kiss my butt." He snarled Hispanic crap. The president smiled "Let's go to Dallas." "We are Cuban not Hispanic."

"Jack Kennedy was happy. The White House staff was happy. Jocky smiled, "Be careful John. The Cuban monastery will kill you with prayers to the Devil." John looked at her. He smiled. "Monastery means monks that served Jesus. There are no Cuban pieces of cap than can take me." The president smiled. He was a charming man when he smiled. "Be careful John, your dads in freezer units. The Cubans are evil at night. Do not anger them, wave and say warfare off." Jocky pecked John on the nose. "Those Cubans are lousy at warfare their numbers go to one trillion, mine to one trillion because I think well. They couldn't one thousand stage one. I want food." The Egyptians smiled and said, "Are you on number one thousand? Be careful. John has a military and a gun for you. Ask Al Capone's involvement tax invasion that he is if he's involved. He will kill you at point blank range do not steal money from Al or his ancestry will come in and claim wave and it goes off daily." The head pharaoh spoke his money was trillions in America. Trillion all day because he invested well. The Cuban one thousand signed at the bottom. It said food. The communist leader was starving. "Dallas" John F. Kennedy said, "When we get there I'll buy you breakfast." The president said to his wife. President John F. Kennedy and his wife arrived in Dallas Texas two hours later. The warnings were none. The event was scheduled political. The United States military, the city police was sparse because they detailed no problem. John F. Kennedy had a high IQ. He tallied people without them knew it. Al caught that he tried playing strategy without being apparent. Al got business through one hundred percent.

Al's business was guns. He sold the United Nations one hundred percent and sold weapons from twelve. President Kennedy bought millions because he thought he has to contend with the black market, a legal service promotion by the United States. The guns were stolen out of the US Army and resold by the black market. Al ran the black market. The reason Al thought the black market was legal was when he was twelve. The president said that you could steal from the army only if you were Al and only if your life depended on it. The weaponry saved Al's life one hundred percent. When the cops move in on Al Capone at age twenty three with no charges.

John F. Kennedy rented a limousine. He and his wife were very tired from the trip. His IQ was extra high, Al sold guns to Cuba. He told them how to use them none, he sold to twenty three countries that day. The Cubans were one thousand. They made it one and a half hours. They took a limousine also. They told the service that they were friends of the president and he would pay. Through time it was seldom that assassins really existed during the Confederacy. Abraham Lincoln believe the Confederacy existed none. The Confederacy contained one hundred percent of the Middle East and armies went through time from the 1800s to present. The south that joined the Confederacy President Lincoln read about the end of time forces in a Book of Mormons that was published by time and said that the Confederacy served the Devil with all of their hearts. The book was out a year and was destroyed by Time. If asked, he did not think the Confederacy existed. He published a paper that said the Confederacy should be contended with because they served Satan not God. The United States military under the little the calvary were one million. He wanted them to come in for warfare. The newspaper was the Los Angeles Tribune released in Los Angeles. Anglo Saxton was one million Mexicans from Mexico live in Los Angeles call Anglo Saxton. They were good for the country because they worked hard. The state's population was ten. The number of people thirty million. Kentucky was woodland one hundred percent. There was no way to get in and out and Tennessee was woodland one hundred percent. There were no streams at the bottom of the Los Angeles tribune. It said the Confederate Army was cowards and served the Devil. President Lincoln wanted them out of commission.

Washington was in New Jersey, there was no New York. General Ulysses Grant looked sixty with a gray beard. He played himself, Jesse James a pig farmer that looked venomous and was forty pounds overweight. If he moved beside your house he killed you one hundred percent of the time with a .38 Smith and Wesson. He wore a false beard and hair that made him look older. "Hi, I'm General Ulysses Grant and wish to sign for warfare under stage 3." He signed Ulysses Grant and may the best man win. It was on with the end of time forces. Ghost from Hell warfare. The second president that Ulysses signed stage 3 with was President Bill Clinton. He did not think the ghost army existed. The Cuban third part to the president and the assassin number twenty three fired on President John F. Kennedy. Who was dropped into freezer units was a nonexistent dummy that existed none that simulated the number of presidents. That was President Bill Clinton, number of presidency the Kennedy's were no relationship to anyone except the Kennedy's. John was deceased.

Al was in the alcohol and drugs. Officer Elliott Ness who said that stage 3 was for Al and he wanted him and his army of a million dead. The Sicilian Mafia numbered one trillion. Elliott Ness's officers were ten, the reason they wanted him dead was tax invasion. He looked at Al and said, "You're under arrest for tax invasion." Al went to the police down the street and said, "Elliot Ness newly appointed drug and alcohol official." Elliott had been there for three weeks. Al told the officer that he said tax invasion and he was clear of those charges, "Can I kill him since he's not a uniformed officer with charges?"

"Yes." The officer replied, "If you present me with the body." Al shot him. He was down a block in front of the Chicago Tribune. He though that he would tell them that Al ran off like a chicken. The shot cracked him in half. Mark Lyons his right hand man took the body and gave it to the officer. The officer said, "Go you're innocent." Because he was not a uniformed officer. Al got by with murder. Al was in Elliott's office when the President John F. Kennedy was assassinated by Cuba. Elliott had two daughters Jill and Rebecca two and four. Their friend was a two year old named Jennifer. Elliott left them alone when he was out. He fed them every two days. Their mother died of a drug overdose one month after Jenifer the two year old was born. She was pre-scribed medicine by the doctor she took too much and died. Their kids went up for adoption.

John F. Kennedy's brother Bobby was inaugurated president two hours after his brother's death. He took the oath and swore vengeance on the killer of his brother. The Cuban were in row boats with paddles heading back to Cuba. They went one mile. They in the airport at Singapore in the one hour. Newly appointed President Bobby Kennedy clocked in for the presidency. Fast Eddie was an accountant for their mom. He was forty pound over weight and the mob could take a city out in minutes with warfare techniques. "Are you after the mafia?"

Time Impairment

Hi, we're Egyptian. We are newly established and we go against the other only when they go to God and leave us out. Erving Moses was my brother, he was Jewish and we raised him. He changed our output, we still served the same. We respect Moses the same as a brother. He changed nothing.

The Egyptian pharaohs wore robes, their heads were shaven and they were in a monastery praying. Their robes were white as snow. Egypt had a population of one trillion, one billion times. The men were billions of soldiers with guns and knives that killed, when the pharaoh was in danger. The succeeded 100 percent of the time. Egypt was very miraculous with future everywhere It took trillions of years to build Egypt. There were no organizations the Egyptians could not take over. They were prudent at all eras of life with one exception. They served God now.

Egypt was very old and good at trade with other countries. They were good at warfare, taking over organizations and were a B level of Egypt. It was very much the future. The pharaohs ran Egypt 100 percent. Cleopatra was one of a million princesses that ran a portion of her father's estates. She was his favorite because she was pretty. The pharaohs were very educated, their IQs were high. It showed in some biblical way. The Egyptian Empire was taken seriously as apposition. It looked well or bad a long, long time ago when Moses went against the Egyptian Empire; one against a notation. He was known to be a family member however and was very welcome in Egypt, and could weather perverse or not. State that he was a brat that was in an adoptive family, which knew system of his family that raised him. He caused things to happen in an empire than he knew the systems of an empire that he was very welcome in and note. To take away the parables of God, for they were known to work for humans not against ideas expressed in stories was to enhance the cognitively of mankind, not take away.

Egypt was very well educated and very evil. They said Moses mattered none because they were not against Moses. They main Pharaoh who was over Egypt Erving Stature, he was Moses adopted brother and very powerful in world trade. He traded with no bones about it. His money was great. Egypt was and empire that was known well in the United States as a Middle East country. The power structure and authority was and is the same. Egypt showed up and the pharaohs owned Egypt and were very college educated. The language was the same English the United States spoke. They knew no better than to wear robes and to be priest of the devil. There was no pettiness; it was how they were raised in the Middle East. The Egyptians spoke well, and their kids were raised educated in the world affairs. Their communities had future, they lived very well. The Egyptians had trade 100 percent because they knew how to trade was issued.

Trade meant service earlier in time. Egypt knew how to feed their country and keep a water supply and cloth themselves. Their education and high trade meant the country paid for food and turned orders issuing tee food needed to keep the country feed. The Middle East grew food poorly, they never learned how. They phoned in orders if got it, they got it and they paid full price. They went underground seldom and called the shots for ever because they modified Satan. I'm smocks and promoted Satan their heads were shaven, they knew no better than to modified Satan. It was the same through earlier time to present. The pharaohs were the same. The Egyptians of the Middle East were very evil priest of Satan. Some had shaved heads and they knew how to take over business' 100 percent of the time.

Cleopatra was Erving Statures daughter. She was known to be one percent; a son would be 100 percent and add to the Egyptian Empire. What Erving Statures regretted was the God saw her because she was made immortal by the principles of Jesus in Judas priest of America into the future. She was regarded as a nun and Muslim of judicial statute; a princess of the highest regard. She was educated by Erving Stature in the Egyptian empire and was a daughter to the throne of Egypt, not a son. Erving Stature would frown at a daughter and smile to have a son she'll do. He smiled well, praised he the Egyptian way. He palace was worth trillions. Cleopatra was a princess only because Erving Stature was the head ruler over Egypt. They were number one in crime.

Al Capone lost because he said Jesus and pointed, they said you serve Jesus was Erving Stature. I ruined Al Capone because he was branded a fanatic of Jesus, he served no one. He was never taught how. He was saying that Egypt served Jesus because he saw Cleopatra at an airport handing out stickers that said Jesus. She saw Al Capone and said, "Jesus, I serve Jesus, you serve Jesus." Al smiled and truth fully stated, "I serve no one." He had a derringer .38 trained on security and shot one guard because he modified currency wrongfully and called him sir. He ran and he looked like James Rockford with dark eyes like a cobra. People misunderstood courtesy for Christian ways.

He was devoid of kindness because he was out on tax evasion one second of his life and got it back two. He cared nothing about Jesus of God because he was tax devoid. 100 percent upon saying Jesus he went zero amongst the Egyptians 100. He was talking about Cleopatra. She was told about Jesus and after she served Satan she offered Al Capone a sticker. He refused; she smiled and stuck on a car, a 1928 Desoto. It was then years ahead of its time, the stickers twenty. She knew that she ruined Al at the peace talks with America 1977, before the Olympic Games. Erving Stature stated, "Go Al Capone or I will kick your butt and kill your ancestry." Al Capone had trained a .38 on Erving Stature. He would have gone to freezer units and told Al Capone ancestry that he was a Jesus freak. He would have dispersed Al Capone pictures as a ruin at a religious convention, a Baptist church and said that he served Jesus at the service.

Al killed half the church because they spoke of sacrificing his ancestry to the devil. He was the only mafia that killed Italians. True the only. After Erving Stature dispensed the pictures, he would have been killed by Al Capone. He went to the freezer units and returned in a trillion years, Egypt would have followed him 100 percent. Cleopatra would have been killed by Erving Stature at 80 and said, "I wish you were a box Al Capone." Al Capone would have been killed by the Bush administration with two guns to his head by a deputy Louis Clark of Pittsburg. Bull his right hand man held the gun and said, "Do you serve Jesus or God?' He would state neither honestly and be killed by Bull.

"Is he in freezer units?" "NO", Banchi announced. The mafia would have applauded he went out on tax evasion at 66 and followed Satan without knowing it. Al's money spent was one trillion a thousand times. His tax evasion was of in a second and he earned money legally. His occupation was black market gun deals. He knew no better than to be good with hun demonstrators because he wanted to sell them. After Al stated Jesus he went to zero and never reclaimed.

Cleopatra never explained that she was kidding about the stickers. The Egyptian Empire was one trillion, one billion times. The Sicilian Mafia was one trillion in freezer units under Al Capone. He was a crack. Usually, he killed the leader and took over the organization. Usually he won. If he would have killed Erving Stature he would have returned in one trillion years. The reason Al Capone ran when he saw the Egyptians was because he said, "You serve Jesus", Cleopatra and it's a ruin for you. He ran and left them alone.

Egypt was very powerful in numbers. One in crime, their criminal affairs was they could take over businesses and kept it forever. They gave it up rarely, only if the parents cried and said, "Please give it back." Religion was settled usually before business currency was currency. If legal in the United States, it was legal and you were protected by the law. Region was written and wars did not depict religion. You were fed by legal workmanship. Stature and Egypt knew no better than Satanism, usually people were not bothered. If workmanship was high and they bothered nobody in America. Organizations were supposed to promote you or your product and be legal.

Erving Stature saw God and admitted that he was all powerful. His mistake was that he did not wipe Egypt out. He was high in IQ. Stature, Erving was upon stating we lost nothing and Moses is back among our tribe. He was a Jewish man with a beard raised about thousands of pharaohs that returned to Egypt. He stated "Stature Erving we lost nothing."

New York school was crack. They taught Egyptian some, mummification and embalming of the Egyptian Empire. Steve Thompson was intrigued by the Egyptian digs and ruined. He taught history and he knew the history taught Jesus none. He wondered why the ruins were not looked for in Jesus, a being of the profits. He would have found that twelve disciples buried in the sand of Egypt Jerusalem, down deep in the sane. The twelve profits were killed by the Egyptians of poison. School systems thought that if you taught about Jesus you should speak about how to overcome Satan. In all disguises determine Jesus as a profit of saint of God and why he was crucified instead of spoken about his way of life. The tribes of Satan were the twelve disciples that turned Jesus into Rome. Jesus was found in eternity, Jerusalem was sank trillions of leagues under the sea. He won 100 percent of the time. God because he was all powerful. Jerusalem was ruined into Jesus that was black, delivered from Africa. Jesus rose to heaven, the disciples were in hell.

The way the turned was they stated poison for Jesus. Egypt applauded and upon his death and mourned Satan's lose in eternity. Religion meant to the state department, the education of a male pastor that took over a congregation. That meant a church full and they were called sheep untold that the weak inherited eternity and the war of Satanism was on the minister. He would set you on fire to serve God. The minister was make and anointed by God. The service was free unless you tithe. Give God what's God's through petty cash. The United States was a freedom of religion yet we as American felt safer if they did not profess Satan as their Lord. They did not know if they would make it to the other side. Evil could take them over and kill them. Religion was cleared by the state department.

Steve Thompson taught history. He was a professor variety. His wife's name was Machale. He was smart and worded history correct. The wars were taught from the war of the states to the Gulf War. The films depicted the wars recreated events. He was strict and prompt. He work up to a full breakfast and liked speaking to his wife Machale, he respected that she was smart. What society had output the most in industry and warfare outside of the United States; we had dictators such as Adolf Hitler. A war that was fought and a great general Douglas MacArthur brought the United States back with the United States military concerning Adolf Hitler's evil rivalry on the world. On the test the most progressive at war that went against our country civilized yet a trained military with an air force, navy, army and marines.

The commercials on television incorporated and educated a military that has output in police action protection in world trade we were good since the cavalry fought the confederate army. We looked at the enemy and stated that our protection units were high assignment. Look at the index and contact the biggest military of all time. A hand was raised Ricky Adams. Steve the professor states, "Stay with the topic, I have not asked four questions." "Mr. Thomas why would we random war zones though a history book of a multitude of pages, and if I may ask was the Armageddon processed in these pages of warfare," Ricky Adams the sixteen year old student asked Steve Thompson wrote the assignment on the board. Write the assignment down, the teacher looked at the student "What if it was our country of warfare and richness that was tired of having God as a dictator? We thought that we never asked to be created. We didn't want to answer to God anymore but to govern the universe ourselves. What army would you select as our Armageddon, a complete overtake of God." "I don't know Mr. Thomas, someone fierce and unexpected." "Where sirs do you think the archives exist, perhaps in the Middle East?" Steve Thompson asked.

The teacher was born in New York; he was fluent in facts documented by the state. He knew the boundaries, he was good. Steve Thompson looked at the student and told the truth. The archives and lost world are documented in the bible. It's another state whether super sitcom of focal academia. That's where you find the true documentations of the archives and the lost world, the blood enemies and the countries rise and fall. The bell rang and Steve Thompson stated, "Do not forget the work assignment." One period was over, one hour another class would begin another period and would file Steve Thompson. Grading papers, instructing, the holidays, he taught well, he was well liked.

He stated, "I'm one of his classes the difference in wars of religions and ordinary wars the bible and testament were usually written and the bi laws. Wards didn't changes things. I'm God or Satan the covenant to God. Your output and the national security was that in a life time established. By your choices and behavior toward job relationships, warfare, sports, politics, schools and state offices usually kept going on. Laws and bi laws were set. The military kept foreign over takes out, the police did well on prevention of criminal over takes and the state department tried to feed the hungry.

New York, New York the city the state was filled with trillions of people, the televisions showed stop lights teaming with pedestrians the city was known to be the biggest in the world. The statistics were spoken of; the school teachers spoke of it from a location that had buildings that went far into the clouds and civilization. By day and by night the city came to life with a neon glow. The education was high. In most people's mind was crime was high. In New York was the Sicilian Mafia under that don that ran the city. Crime was only when they went against don. The soldiers maker certain his orders were carried out. They protected the don only.

Steve Thompson received the work assignment and handed papers back graded. The wars lost by the United States none, our progress in trade international was good, and our state department was educated well. In the right eras and trained as well. Stetson Wallace wore a cap; he was navy that was straight. He was lookout for incoming ships. He has a crew and was in charge of keeping warfare ships from coming in and checking cargo out for legal and illegal. He hated the name Stetson because it was a hat. He had a big ego, as big as any acting in the movies. He was strict because he didn't know any better. He was trained to know to. I don't know if I like my job or not, I'll have to ask the president. He reported to the military and asked if there any gays in the military. He looked at them with more charisma than most males and states "I can't." He was like a cop he stated before they got their licensed shops to shore of cargo carries. They were explained the laws and the bi laws if citied the were wrong, the navy backed him and the police if he was legal and illegal. He smiled a charismatic smile and stated "You don't call them if you're illegal, I answer to the president."

The Egyptians were shaven priest of the devil. They knew no better than as priest and statesmen of Satan to serve under their dark prince. The Egyptians lived through time, much of the time throughout that Egypt came and went and all that was left was ruins. They grew their hair back sometimes, others remained bald. Their charisma was high and their output. Stetson had men day in and out keeping an eye on ships coming in. Stetson had a house that was extra nice. It was a captain of the Navy's house, expensive with details of a full bar, benefit serving. It had wanderlust aquariums. The National Geographic Navy, the overtake of Hawaii, World War 2, and wanderlust and plant life it was designed expensive house kept it clean. He like it none because he did not have anything to do with it. The house was listed under navy.

In the phone directory he was the same in most people's eyes as a sergeant of private of military stock, which meant he knew where everything went and was very social at social events. His wife Angela was a dole. The two connected well. He visited her in her Pennsylvania home where the go and learn how to behave when your husband was a navy man. She respected that Stetson cared about his house that had a military office none because it belonged to the navy. He liked having banquets and parties to see the command of the United States military and their wives. He cared none about meetings that ran past his bed time. He would sleep only a couple of hours and be on time for his shift. Boat docks bothered him none, he was an advanced swimmer. Work detail was a full military shift. He stayed in his housing and barracks during business. He saw his wife occasionally and checked ships coming in 100 percent. When it came time for sleep he bolted his house. He has cameras that were heat sensitive that he bought in the compound. He had men on standby. Almost heat sensitive that were alerted if anyone showed up unannounced.

Security brought in the enemy only while Stetson hid and his men went unnoticed. Stetson's house was bolted. Security was automatic with new shift change a bugle call. Stetson shipped out of the back door. He walked behind the house and disappeared. The cameras picked him up none. He was only level b which meant basement entrance. There was none in the enemy's eyes. It was a full house built by him on off time. He called a constructor, a company and showed up on their day off and used their equipment and constructed it unseen, when the men were on leave. It was Saturday and borrowed electricity from the main house that he liked only as an office. His hunt as he looked at it had electricity, phone service, bath and everything needed. It was not listed. The electric showed up none or the phone service. His bed was comfortable and he was secure. He had cameras of security and everything needed of a nights rest. His hut was cozy and he stayed here most every night for security purpose. He slept well. The air conditioning was comfortable and when needed the heat. Bugle call was responded to the nearest town. Autumn day harbor had hotels for the ships, and flights for those broken down with fives or that needed construction. The towns flourished well and were complete.

Stetson burned off a lot of excess calories during a day he kept security during his checking out cargo and invasion ships. Carrying a live gun was intimidating to people were law enforcement agents that would carry are none because of the weapons discharging Stetson knew the military procedure well because he was trained well. Stetson was of sorts your average they called them gunnies. They wore hard hats and reported to the sergeant with the exception that he was a captain of the United States Navy. He smoothed into banquets and pulled hours d'oeurves off the tray. He had a programmer that worked hours on an ego. It was a device that collected your grades, and output your environment coded in for extensive and exotic Hawaiian bar. The environments was high or environment of Halloween. Thanksgiving, Christmas. The environment stimulated your mind in output. For example, your favorite movie of actor and your persona match. A dream stage meant you went under the ocean of Atlantis and became and aspect. It chased away apparitions and placed you on a good standing with yourself. In your own output an ego was one thing that programmers placed together for Stetson another computer program got Stetson in and out of locations. A car would somehow make it or not if the location called for automobile. If he wasn't there do not explain yourself. The programmers were known to be really up for the military.

Stetson was very progressive with system working for him. He was his wife on some weekends. Stetson flight was semi jet that glided through time. I used it for navy purposes only he had a full team of navy programmers and one million fully trained men under him. He was prudent with ships coming and going with cargo. The military radar picked up every war ships. The inferred was advanced year after year. It went beyond dreams into classification of the United States military outlet of the Navy. The education was high and training well adapt.

The United States military was a very powerful country in trade. The output was high in industries in food and the protection of the citizens was high with the police, military and 100 percent of the state department. From education to already mentioned law enforcement, medical, education and all faucets and divisions of the United States department. First the head of the state department usually knew their area of job title from the captain of the police, to the biggest brigadier general. The state department tested and gave titles in these areas after being educated and trained. The United States usually had output in these areas.

Hi, I'm Senator McDowall from Georgia. The president is very, very angry with me for being me. I want democrats to support the fact that he is not. The congressmen cleared out, he apologized for being smart and reversed it the next time and want no votes or electoral for democrats from Delaware. He was sad because the president was very disappointed that he was against big tactics. He was as straight as Lee Majors from the Six Million Dollar Man. The fall guy and the big valley to serious. The president hair was brown; he viewed the White House pleasantly. He was down on his third term, his chances of reelection was good. He moved around and stayed busy in other areas. His IQ and output was high.

The country was opposed of the president 100 percent. This bothered him immensely because he wanted to be liked. The country was against him 100 percent, the state the same. They thought that he was an idiot and a buffoon. The president looked over and at the city considering he saw a Mexican restaurant named Margaritaville. The lights were lime green with an outlet and design of a margarita, a pitcher was pouring a cold lime margarita into a chilled glass. The outline lie up blue ice cubes, green was the color change, then grey. The ice cubes and a pitcher of silver gin or vodka with a green olive disappeared and a margarita was poured into a glass. The neon video was stimulating and had fluorescent environment for the eye retina. It stimulated with neon color. The Margaritatville sign flashed. It was cool colors and environment that took commercials to a comfortable setting. The president saw civilizations, businesses.

The Late Show with Kelly Demarco, he had frizzy brown hair. Kelly Demarco was a late night phene that ate speed and got by with it because he asked for the stimuli variety that did not kill. Axle Rose of Guns and Roses promoted a grave yard shirt and went around to White Castles and ask if anyone was after the Mafia don that he was employed by. He ate White Castles as if it was compatible. He dressed like a companion of Charles Manson and a rattlesnake. They said he took an overdose of speed, he died at 3 a.m. one morning and showed up for his shit the next night. The police investigated to see who died off The Guns and Roses release twenty years ago. I don't know what they found. Kelly advised the president, the room booed.

So, the president knew no better than to modify tax increases no kick back or that some exotic babe from some exotic island tied him down and took away his man hood. The military base was phoned when the president missed a trade meeting and Cuba wanted food. Upon moving in he found our commander in chief tied down wearing her clothes. The president's office was immaculate. His wife was sitting across from the president waiting to have lunch, "You had such a relationship on me in the Bahamas" she state, "Are you through with that?" She was a very disgusted woman. Her hair was blonde, she was different because he husband was younger in appearance and she was younger also. Her build was very good. The president wore a very expensive suit and looked at his wife. I was dead asleep when I woke up I was wearing women's apparel. I said I was sorry; the oppositions will have a field day with it. It ruined you. No I didn't ruin me, it cause a couple of hours of controversies and the military came in and took the ropes off.

The president looked at his wife and said "Am I forgiven?" She smiled "You are forgiven" she said. "Let's go get something to eat" he said with a smile on his face. It was Washington Deli the president went inside. The special was one mile sub, cola, and chips. Upon seeing the president the sub shop cleared out. The sub make looked out "Hi sir, Tim Byers the president, please clear out, you were very kinky on trade was tied up and left incomplete, foreign trade didn't make it go." He wore a white cap and plastic gloves. President Byers was astonished, "This is my wife, and trade went through foreign." President Byers stated. "Go we don't need your business, your ruined, and go."

The president was addressed as the highest commander and chief. He dressed the part, his suit was expensive, his cologne presidential. "Come on slide me a couple of the subs, a mile long, and a cola." He was very persuasive. He got two subs and they ate at a park a couple of blocks away. The president bit into his sub. "Your ruined Tim. You have to come up with something. You went to zero from one hundred," said his wife. "I'm not worried, trade went through, and this is a sandwich." He winked at his wide food was clinging to his teeth, "I'll win you will see."

Kelly Demarco Late Show, the audience applauded. "The president got an overseas call and could not accept it. He was all tied up some Caribbean babe with the body that knocked foreign trade got his credit card and bought one of the foreign countries. Mrs. Byers, the president's wife flew to Hawaii, put suntan oil on and enjoyed a tour guide. She'll be in a romance novel now." The crowd booed. Kelly looked over the crowd, "Why would you boo me, I boo you. Boo." He smiled, his hair was frizzy, he continued on with basketball. The audience applauded. "So you like basketball. Basketball centralizes the United States you like it or hate it. Yet during basketball games you could work out and go play basketball." A big guy states, "I can do both, don't schedule me." "Okay you can. Basketball centralizes high school and college, and what you miss out on is prizes any time. There is an event that centralizes you, get something you can take home or watch that intitules you to a prize. A president ties me up doll or something." The audience applauded and the show went to commercials.

The scenarios went on; humor show showed a double of the president tied up to the railroad tracks while a train came toward him. Senators told jokes, the military stated, "We reframe, he's a good mane." The police told the same. The country spoke indefinitely about the affair. They laughed and joked. The president was ridiculed highly.

High the president's form is something kinky, kinky, and kinky. The senator from Boston spoke, "Give me money, give me reform, give me sex, and give me sex bondage." The crowd of 500 applauded. The president dropped him on every political account, senators laughed and the president's predicament. The President Tim Byers looked out the window. It was time to live or die. He lifted a finger, his IQ was high "Get Cuba on the line." It's Cuba, Fidel Castro, he was saying yes. Warfare tactics would help the economy of America and Cuba would eat. "Okie dokie you got it cowboy," Fidel Castro smiled as his age showed to President Byers. "Give them the snake treatment, anacondas, and all." Fidel smiled, "I am an old man yet I aged through time well." President Byers smiled, "Okie dokie you got a war."

The war was underway with Cuba, the Cuban ambassador was warned the Cuban administration was warned all Cubans knew and came out of the freeze containment. "Hi, I am President Byers, Cuba signed for warfare. Fidel Castro signed. We are at war," President Byers stated. "The whole country was taken underground at gunpoint," President Byers said please and scrambled back to the White House. He was in complete control of trade and could end the war at any time by giving Cuba food. President Byers ate gourmet foods because people ate gourmet foods at special occasions and this was special.

The underworld or a hostage camp for the United States citizens were full of cubicles full of citizens' old, young, male, female, kids and babies. The overtake was Cuba. They had weapons and asked for government protocol who the Cuban knew the language barely is government protocol. The Cubans were named number from one to trillions we don't need a name. The were evil, against America when food was refused from the president. The president sat in his oval office, his wife and family was frozen. The military did a good job and was frozen too. The F.B.I was automatic, the state police frozen; their output was high against organized crime. Cuba was the overtake; they had future systems to look like the United States. They were against the country because of food. The place weapons to the heads of leaders and threatened to pull the trigger. The leader was scared of none because they thought they were kidding. Cuba would have killed them if they tried to leave.

One hundred percent of America turned to ninety nine percent upon Stetsons waking up. He brewed coffee and picked up recorded messages. His wife called he had visual. She was very pretty. He listened to the messages from his commander, his job performance on ships and cargo was high. He activated the visual of his navy base, there were not any men patrolling, the night shift must have slept. A court marshaling charge for him meant being sent home with charges unbecoming of military.

He had twenty messages. His wife left two. He smiled and shined. He really like her. "Hey Stetson," she spoke into the phone, "When you visit next weekend I have prepared a list of over one hundred jobs for you," he smiled. "Okay maybe I'll let you get by with it if you're nice." The door opened and the Cuban administration entered with weapons. Stetsons' wife was held at gunpoint and brutally raped. Stetson went to fear. She was raped and her clothes lay on the floor. The Cuban leader of ten shot her, her body taken out by the Cuban military. The Cuban average height was five feet nine inches. The leader spoke in Cuban it sounded, in a language intangible. The Cubans brought in a double; she was the spitting image of his wife. The recorder stated no new messages. The phone messages that were left for Stetson were played. They were prerecorded. Cuba left no traces upon killing and leaving doubles. You could tell no difference, there were just that good at what they did.

The navy were frozen with the military. Stetson was the only exception. He knew that his wife was dead. He liked her a lot, some processed love, some convince, and others romance and love. He wanted her alive. Stetson was very taken aback; he was geared for an output with ships coming in to make certain that no deceased goods came in, or illegal cargo of drugs etc. Independent flights could carry drugs in from import to import according to entry and reentry into foreign countries on independent flights from estates. Weather phones and jets were caught fueling and refueling or entered foreign air in and out of foreign air force and landed with drugs. Usually, law enforcement came in uniformed cops, and they used drugs none, they knew the harmful effect and chose not to get high. It slowed them down mentally one hundred percent.

Stetson had been awake twenty minutes. He would have the worse day of his lie if he didn't consider well. In America if divorced your remarried too quick and detailed well. It seemed hot or cold up or down. The point was you were remarried. The kids were usually opposed. His wife died in warfare. He like her well. Stetson was not dressed, he wore boxers. He drank coffee with a nutty flavor some would like it or hate it accordingly. Maybe your breakfast didn't agree with it or coffee straight was a coffee for a males system. I do not commercialize product the manufacturer does, they know by sells. The coffee was a Star Buck chocolate almond with cream, a regular that woke him up well.

Stetson opened the computer in his military office in his main office. He pushed a button and entered into the computer lock frozen. He was frozen in freezer units independent. The form of self his impression and body was high in output with equal strength to out with his navy experience and military record. That way he didn't over play a mood and his experience would equal output. Stetson could get into any location he filed sexual away because he wasn't ready for it. His wife died in warfare with Cuba, he was not informed of the way. His body was video perform and he filled the freezer until of his original.

Egypt ruled like a serpent most thought that they came and went and a new ancestry was in administration. The old ministry was in command and claimed for Egypt what was Egypt. Al Capone was crime; he served no master, upon seeing Cleopatra one of one trillion princesses in a society dominated by pharaohs. She was lost because she was documented. Egypt knew no better than to be priest for Satan, Al viewed Cleopatra as one that served Jesus. He was usually correct; however Cleopatra served Satan she knew no better. The Egyptians knew better none they related all of their experience to Satan, good and bad and never repented. Al was criminal and served none other than money.

Religion usually was not pronunciation in warfare because the bible was already written and warfare did not change the contents of the bible. Your output in the state service was yours, the military was its self, and the police intervened only if they found you illegal.

Here you go Steve. The sixteen year old Steve Thompson received pay from a family business. He smiled and placed the money in his pocket. He environment was Indian because his girlfriend was Indian at seventeen. Her build was an A. He was good looking somehow the environment was created. It was also sweet seduction cherry blossoms of a teen that was pretty and kept a torn for a savage look of sensual and pretty. Him and her were crazy about each other and drank of the tranquility of sex nightly.

"Marry me," Teresa Redman proclaimed. "I cannot because I do not have a stable job." The couple Teresa Redman and Steve Thompson at seventeen used the house of their parents up for a year. They were gone most every night, for a year Steve was at a family souvenir shop waiting for Teresa. He was in her dad's office upon filling and leasing the computer. It scrolled the items of the souvenir shop and stated Indian burial ground freezer units. Steve typed in freeze me. He was frozen. By a fluke five minutes later the United States was hostage in cubicles. The aggressor was the confederate army. The confederate army looked like the United States from seas to shining sea. Teresa was frozen by hostels.

Hi, I am Patty, Patty Smith, I am Teresa's replacement. Her face was pretty, her chest small and she said that she was Teresa Redman. I am F.B.I. Her training was I don't look like me. I look like her. The confederate army from the south and from hell was the takeover. Their demands were that they wanted to be treated with respect down here. They received on million dollars, seven years later and went back to freezer units. Hell was aflame. The confederacy was somehow a world that existed whether from Saddam and Gomorrah of the past. A society chose Satan and was marked. It was a big society and after receiving the mark of Satan, society went on the takeover was military police and government. The police moved in on Christians and made certain they were brought in; Gods wonderment went upon serving Satan in any capacity. The fowl came in of the planet because society had no protection. The fowl was serpents from hell.

The confederacy was a complete takeover of a country in warfare during this time. They were hostages of the United States. The president signed for warfare. The United States money was processed. The army from hell took over and looked like the United States. People were starved if they spoke from hostage cubicles underground. They were processed by the F.B.I. confederate army. It was thirty years earlier upon returning, the United States was happy. The way did not make the paper. Steve Thompson gained seven years of his life upon being released from freezer units. The Indians dad Teresa Redman Blackwood stated, "It's been seven years, it's over with Teresa. I really liked you Steve. Go." Steve ran and ran; his mom, dad and family were seven years older. Teresa Redman was deep in chronological sleep not to rest any recall, the double was F.B.I. and an enemy to her family and to Steve Thompson. Steve Thompson taught history. He graded the papers and handed them back. Warfare teachers were based and caused by stock and product from the United States being discontinued by the president.

He went into the wars, the confederacy to the Gulf War. One thing that wasn't spoken of was the Abraham Lincoln died in a war zone and JF Kennedy died during a Cuba crisis. Steve Thompson was up most of his day during the 80's. They stated that you juiced, they had blenders that broke fruit down and vegetables. In the movies it showed Sylvester Stallone placing raw eggs in a blender and drinking them down wilderness was mapped out and if smart had a rest room facility. Usually classified were guys that wanted to be rugged and enjoy the great outdoors. The United States state department was usually pretty good at placing signs upon a location that was bad for mankind. Usually people wanted to go where the ambulance and police could run for the sake of injury.

Egypt had super sitcom what happened to the old world of pharaohs and mummification was their caves. The Egyptians would state there are lots of caves in Egypt all over and there were trillions of caves in Egypt. They went in them none because we did not want to get wet. Steve Thompson wrote Egypt, Atlantis and ten cost worlds. Egypt was none of the dawn of time. It was relieved that the old world of Egypt died. The Egyptians rated number one in criminals. They came in when it states the Egyptians name and collected. They killed with guns, some they collected one hundred percent. When Egypt was spoken of wrongfully Steve Thompson reflected on he moved as a kid of twelve to another location upon asking his grade he stated eighth instead of seventh. A principle tried failing him because he and some friends missed a day of classes and went to a wood area.

Fort Haven, Bob Yogun a doctor from a school system asked that I got to a New Haven School and fail Steve Thompson. He lied to the school system about his grade. Bob was straight army. He was AAA at nothing. I don't know about a kid, let him go I want him the principle hand punched Bob stated. Sid went into treatment previously years ago for too much gin. He recovered and stated that he was homosexual. That was an out for the neutral army man that swayed no sex preferred. He was out on that one and reentered another occasion. Sid was navy in his town, by excuse he asked no one from the military go there and he wore a tattoo that reminded people of a sailor. He was an army alcohol counselor. He states retirement from the navy and still active on base. Sid Logan was liked by no one in his hometown because they thought that he was homosexual. He has no sexual. Bob got in a as teacher, Steve Thompson grade was a C from his previous school, a passing grade. The principle Casy wanted to fail him for missing class and presented no charges. Bob failed him. Billions of students failed at one time. The education system conned none if you were no in a grade they tell you. Bob rode with a staff of people on Steve Thompson and one thousand teachers states to the future educator of history eighth grade. Bob the eighth grade teacher was zero. The military man could not read and write Steve gained some now even repeating the eighth grade.

The darkness and black magic from a presidential pentagon computer that the president activated permeated the mind. The country would be subjected to complete warfare. The process would enable the presided to process memory. The Middle East became war zones against the United States one hundred under Satan for at least a hundred years. Their warfare was high and the Middle East wanted to make it through time.

The B.O.B. Underground City

The educator from New York skimmed through programs, a 70 Z Egypt was modified a secretive society hence forth if the data pronunciated. The Egyptians syllables were pronunciated even tone with output American was somewhat cowboy theatrical and output. The 1980 Bruce Willis in Die Hard was a cop in and out of uniform. Nicotine was dispensed and the state department left you alone on lung cancer was preventative by not smoking. The officer Joh McClain could avoid foreign prosecution if he was foreign in their countries and saw somebody doing something if he asks is that legal. The American cowboy variety of male withdrew from communism be dead, yet people from the Middle East were very civil in America. That was not a war zone at the time. The Middle East was for America on trade. The wore robes that modified Rabbis of Satan. They were extra friendly in warfare; they were high trade for foreign usually went because the Middle East was called names that were prejudice. The sales were high, they ate food. Two countries modified insect of larva. Cuba was one, A to Z Middle East warfare.

The country was not certain of the hostage situation. It was spoken of none because of fear of a reoccurrence. Cuba was brutal at warfare and went unnoticed. The country got their stomach full of fruit, and went into freezer units the country came out on a B. The memory was taken out of eating larva, as a B replacement ate it. The reason foreign were good at warfare was because they knew no better, they had to protect themselves. The Egyptians modified output without arrogance or hostility. There were good at warfare, and were very educated. They grew angry seldom, and had high output. They knew how to speak to Americans. They did not get into John Wayne communism against Satansim The John Wayne ways of life was to Egypt arrogance with no backing. The United States military trained well against the enemy. The police were trained to abstract crime out.

The teacher listed wars A to Z from Egypt to Germany and the Gestapo. Stetson ordered coffee and a breakfast biscuit. She had the same except a mocha, and glass of water. Her name was Timmy, her build was very nice. Stetson asked that she prepare herself fully dressed. He smiled, a pig is only a farm animal. About the only time school teachers etc. call someone a pig is when they have eaten too much, a teach, "Do you mind if I speak of schools?", "Absolutely just don't tell me how to dress." She held the phone. Teachers speak how they want, yet are hired by the state. If the do not like something that someone states they will try to change the curriculum. The test on the view of the student because teachers do not want bosses, what they don't change is Webster's Dictionary only when it's been revised.

"I know that you think well, I will dress fully, we will talk until one a.m. after all I'm your cousin." "I mean nothing by it," Stetson smiled. "I just do not want fights." "I know." Timmy stated. "No car wrecks. I know you're my cousin, I'm not a pig?" Stetson asked. "I agree a pig is a farm animal, your my cousin." Timmy stated. Stetson sat down, Timmy did also. She was very pretty and dressed fully, mean no swim in the pool with a quick towel and a dive in demine or swim wear. In which her cousin Stetson was submitted into mena friendly her desirable and he felt like because men came onto her and she was his cousin not his date. He like her immensely. He collected information that was going on in his life and asked questions about hers. She smiled and kept up to date with the conversation.

The Cubans were set aside from Cuba, and educated to appropriate English and manners. The Cubans received high marks and their output was college. They were given Egypt one day in Greenland and adapted Egypt as their own. They would be confused as Hispanics. Today their personalities were out going. Upon shaving their heads they looked like kids for ten years. They grew up with mascaraed and tactics they were original Egyptians. The true race of Cuba, which spoke Cuban only.

Stetson smiled, it's been forever since conversation made sense. Timmy was very pretty and like Stetson a lot. Conversation is important to process the should and mind. You think better if you like someone she took a drink of her beverage. "You should be a private detective, you have a military mind, and you could catch up with law enforcement classes." Stetson smiled, "I would like that. I may use that idea for an outlet for a job that pays.

Stetson set up a detective agency after receiving his license. He had a good military mind and was very collective on where things belong. In the military he was mostly for people his output was high. He placed his number in the phonebook wondering if he shouldn't be more secretive and more of a spy about it. Before taking on a client he would look the credentials over and keep it legal. He didn't want to advertise yet Stetson hung his single out as a private detective after completing criminal law and receiving his licenses. He wanted business and cases and he wanted the alone feeling to go way that he had since Cuba slay his wide. Stetsons single read: Stetsons Detective Agency. The office was rented and furnished because the furnishings and board room would have cost a lot. The office chairs were thick cushions and cozy. His phone system and after hour's answering service was attached. He was ready for clientele.

Stetson funded a banquet. It was Timmy's idea to promote the detective agency. He handed out cards and served banquet foods. He hated it yet promoted himself and the detective agency. He hired a band that played tantalizing Hawaii and exotic location music and presented a bar. Stetson can't figure it out" and he shirt and "no one can" a promotion of Stetson agency. He smiled and spoke well. The servings were grilled hot dogs and hamburgers and BoBBS with beef and pork saturated in sweet and sour sauces of Hawaii. The outside buffet was full of beef stewed potatoes. The drinks of cola were fountain iced cold.

Stetson had a crowd he didn't know if it was promotional to improve his detective service yet he wanted to make a good impression and work a full eight hour days. "Hi," the crowd silenced. "I'm Stetson, Detective Agency; I was retired navy and trained in the detective agency." Timmy smiled and pointed a thumb at Stetson. She was very pretty. "He's really good," she smiled her skin was brown from sun. "Timmy's my cousin, hopefully I can serve you."

Stetson took his hat off, "I am licensed by the state and would like to help in areas that need to be brought out." Stetson hired a programmer, and she programmed security and probability of teams set up. She could make an environment comfortable after he rented his office and listed himself in the phone directions. Stetson places a good party together with foods that smelled tantalizing, music of Hawaii and wondrous places plus exotic drinks. Timmy smiled, Stetson spoke well the crowd said that they would call if they could not figure something out and needed a private investigator.

America was arrogant against communism from the Russian cosmonauts on into the Gulf War and other Middle Eastern wars. It showed some the Middle East called the John Wayne Syndrome. America won their wars, and had high commodity. The Middle East had no commodity, they placed everything into warfare. America was high in warfare. It was almost as if the sheiks of the Middle Eastern oiled bought oil from America. They could have been known sheek because they were sheek with the woman, smooth and had ten wives. They were eastern women. The sheek were high at warfare. The wars with Egypt were none, they spoke well to the United States and gained commodity. The United States thought that the Middle East was new in generation. They were old in regime and knew the United States thought that the Middle East was new in generation. They were old in regime and knew the United States well. They were college educated in the United States.

Upon being taken hostage when the president let them in, the Middle East would ask if certain American that was known to slurs the Middle East and call them prejudice names. The Middle East seized the United States it was called The End of The United States Regime, or administration president Sidd Byers let Cuba in. The country would not comply and let is exotic vacation go. The whole cabinet was hostage. The military complied and the F.B.I., the United States knew who was responsible none if they tried without being taken hostage underground. Thus laughed and made fun of their slurs and went back to the same. The police was on the side of Law and Order. The United States was repopulated doubles at this time. The Middle East left no sign. The Middle East would ask why prejudice names if they said none and waved side way they let them go. Did you sign for stage games the Middle East would ask, "No", the American would state, "It means the government came through your mind and tested your warfare?" "No, I didn't sign, they start it seldom without a signature if so you wave." He waved and it goes away. They go back, support none; they let it show none, only that don't work for them. They go back on the same pretense and win if they give nothing up. You are an American; I am Middle Eastern person of warfare. If they American hired him he ate in the normal two weeks if not he missed a day.

Timmy stayed around Stetson's house some. She leafed through the mail. "Stetson you have a welcome to your local church," Stetson smiled. "It is the USA yet the temperance may change. The service is state and your output may be good in recognizing sine without an education by the state to promote better drag noises of sin. You're a detective you have a bad representation of God." Stetson smiled. "Did you Timmy show up to my door to be recognized, I'm relative output in banquet for to be known to be pretty." Timmy pushed him, "I come to see you."

Stetson smiled, "Thank you very much. I've saw good work in treatment and state service that had output because people knew how to live and give up habits that was bad." "Yes, but did they confess their sin to God?" "There we have it." Stetson smiled. "I used a program that I strolled into hence forth through this program I learned to withdraw and in my mind I hired a new representative." "Did this organization repent for their sine?" "Look I read a self-help book a long time ago, it was called Unlimited Power, and I like it. I loaned it to someone, along with Think and Grow Rich, Learn Patience, and How to Be a Millionaire." Timmy smiled she was very pretty, "As of not I'm collecting on pretty," she was kidding.

"These books were very inspirational to me." "Self-help is self-help. I don't think you are a millionaire however," Timmy smiled. Stetson looked at her sternly. "I hid in my mind and knew that you thought that I was rich," Stetson looked at her sternly "I hid in my mind and knew that you though that I was rich," Stetson scowled. "I never thought that, you don't show it. Those cards glittered on special occasions that I sent you, had reserves, you hid it well." "I did" Timmy smiled, "You could have bought a bunch of well-known in name cards, and you could have bought them at a going out of business sale." "Remember the unicorns and palaces when you were a kid, it showed pretty." "Yes, and I learned the princess did not have a big output in the kingdom. Thanks for the cards." "You don't have to think I'm rich." "No, you are rental like me. That way you can keep systems up by the state." "The states expensive, I was a state employee of the military. I loaned the books to a friend and he tried to pattern his life after me," Stetson said.

"Did he do better or worse?" "They try to extract people's personalities. If they don't give permission, they'll give kid permission that theirs some. I went his way none when he behaved like me." "Who did you behave like, and did they contradict you?" Timmy asked. "I behaved like me. The idea is to pattern healthy habits that others had into your life. You usually use books that your organization approves of in the state department for output on the job. There's free time that you many want to look into other areas." "It's witch craft. If you give someone an unexplained areas that they don't fully understand because their traits in self-help may come out unexplained if specified. The reader of self-help may understand the traits and the output. By the way do you have anything against God?" "No." Stetson said. "I disapprove of people thinking people that dispense religion that they control heaven or hell and not God. You've had people that you preferred none, as representatives. Religion is an aspect that the state controlled with police protection allowing the churches to be legal, the selling of books and evangelist on TV. The ministries were educated by colleges in the United States, whether you believe that a sinless life will promote eternity, there is no proof eternity exists. The people will sometimes claim to go to the devil with that, yet it would prove God's existence with the fallen angel from eternity. I heard someone say that churches stank of death and embalm. That could mean the death and rise of Christ." Stetson smiled.

Instead of stage with Rome or whatever happened the prophets could have gained if they would have spoken to Rome and the Roman leader and given them pamphlets on the alpha and omega or the coming of Christ of it Moses could have gained permission from the lead pharaoh and to open the chapel in Egypt and speak on behalf of God. Jesus was a man the distributed through peace, he taught and really distributed well he was kind and showed no warfare." Stetson smiled. If he could have crossed his fingers. His maid had lived to be ninety. Stetson smiled. "I was only kidding." Timmy helf the invite to church that she found in the mail, "Are you going to church as the invitation invites?" "Yea, I'll go." Stetson and Timmy went Sunday.

The year was 1860. It was a recall of the confederate army. The number one trillion one hundred times crimes. The overtake of the United States the reason. Jed Clampit lost on tax invasion. Jed Clampit was in movie and serious the first was a comedy. The computer processed the confederate army. Jed's success was high. He went through time under an assumed name Jubilee Scakett through through his story the southern battalion of rebellion overtake of an early United States was determined a loss for the south. The confederacy somehow rated one hundred percent in output.

The attorney looked at Jed Clampit. The attorney wore a nice suite and was well groomed. "How do you please?" "Guilty" "That is so," the attorney stated. "That's true," "Any comments?" Jed looked at the attorney; he wore no hat that he usually wore. He had no riddle after tax invasion. He went for nothing good. The other attorney was asked if he had any comments. He went out on tax invasion. "Hell the grave I hit," Jed looked up. "The next time have the devil recreate me."

"Mr. Capone." Yes Al Capone was straight Italian he kind of looked like James Garner a detective in a 1970 series called the Rockford Files. He looked straight Rocky depicted by Sylvester Stallone. Straight Italian Al Capone was brilliant at crime and went after people when they tried taking money from him. They city of Chicago wants your money distributed to the president. Franke Garcia was like his ancestors were Italy. He was a 1920 drug dealer.

"Mr. Capone, drugs excite you, then once addiction set in you need it the rest of your life. It's expensive to be addicted. It takes three weeks to come off. AA works, then you show income that's welfare. The disability is they can't handle things well because they're used to being babied. If you distribute heroin as a stress releaser they will forget about tax invasion an you can steal from them." Al Capone dropped his beverage, hot tea it was imported from Brazil and expensive. It was shipped for a king and Al intercepted it in Egypt, said "We want Al to have his tea." Frankie Garcia brought it in. I lost on tax invasion by going into the wrong office and waiting for my mother I was twenty three. Not I am forty. Al Capone was in freezer units and out on a four it was replica body that Al didn't know the difference of.

"I was in the tax department one second and I spoke only to say wrong office, my mom came in and we went home." Al Capone had two million in the bank and three houses in Chicago. He states legal business it took ten years to accumulate. His business was black market guns. He was cautious during loading. He sold to anyone that wanted to buy. He went from an A to a 4 freezer until. He said, "Why would you want to shoot me, I sold you a gun." He didn't know any better than to sell guns to the public. It was a legitimate business. Kathy Albright said, "You're out of business because you signed for political games under Stage 3 references to the government. Stage means you play the government. If the military comes in just say, I don't play they will leave. If they don't call the police, they play only if they sign. If a national communication opens get everyone to wave sideways and they won't play you on that communication. If they do it twice play them only if the get elaborate on the national communication only. It comes off with death. Death is poison, you on death row by the state police only if you want kids dead. It comes off when you die. The president can take it off. It comes back on if when you die after you signature goes into the state department. For government games you had to sign. Al Capone was ten when he signed for Stage 3 in the state police office. He forgot about it."

Al Capon is out on tax invasion. He went freezer units and was in the tax department on a four. "Break him down", Kathy Albright spoke to the state. They moved in and broke him down and let him go. He had a, 38 pistol. They didn't know they had. Then they were release in ten years for buffalo hunters to make no noise. They cracked loud and buffalos fell dead. The puncture was a quarter and the guts maimed. They came back seldom. You're under arrest for tax invasion, the state police was ten. "Where did you get that .38?" "It was not mine, it's yours." Al gained on that drug dealer's trick; the cop put it on his pocket.

Michael Coulove was there. He won because he had no weapon. He was surprised when Al said "Kill him." He was talking about the head of the state police. Michael looked at Al in handcuffs and stated, "Call Frank he loves you or Lisa your wife." Michael ran out. Al had killed no one at the time; he thought that killing was futile because you could handle things by speaking about it. Kathy Albright stated two million goes back to the state. Two million during the 1920s was equal to one trillion thousands of time. "you signed for Stage 3 at ten." Al stated and they let him go. He went out the door of the tax department, "Your tax devoid Al Capone. You will never earn in the United States."

The meeting was at the Hyatt Regency in Chicago. "Hi, I'm Al Capone. "Hi, I'm Al Capone. I am building an army to overcome tax invasion." Al Capone builds an army of one trillion Italian soldiers. Training was three weeks The Chicago Tribune had a picture of Al Capone. It said Stage 3 Cadet Went Out. Under Al's picture it said tax invasion bill under gained by default candidate Al Capone lost trillions playing money. It showed Al stating I'll take that, it was a poker chip. Al opened Vegas one year later.

What I want you to do is rob my money back and I'll take you through time. Bull will get you out of the situations and into freezer units. Casey Marcum was twenty two and a done and a half. "Good morning Casey," his wide stated. "Hi baby doll you mine forever sex and all." She smiled; she loved "I love you." "I'll kill your oldest kid. Maybeline was her name. Mascara runs but

I'll keep your name forever," she said. She left him in three weeks because it was the late 1920s and they spoke of sex none. She left because he mentioned sex, he thought she was kidding. She was my wife and I thought you could mention it.

Fast Eddie Marcum came in; Case Marcum was Al Capone's brother. He had one trillion mafia soldiers. Eddie was his first cousin. "Are you going to do the police today?" Eddie asked. "Yea, if they come after Al's money", Casey stated. He took a raw egg and ate it because there was no food. "Your wife looks mad." Eddie's job was executioner of the will s for Al Capone's and he bought money back if the police had any charges he told you. He spoke of sex; you don't until the forties when condom banks fill with male for his kid. Eddie smiled. "She's angry really." Eddie wore a hat and was straight Italian. "The women consider you an ugly duckling because you're fat, too fat to fry." Eddie was forty pounds overweight. He ate what was wasted why, "Because I don't want to pay for food." Fast Eddie Marcum smiled, "I may be ugly but I'm not a duckling." Fast Eddie was talking to Maybeline.

"If you lost weight they would swoon. "Tell Al I want to leave my husband upon speaking of male wrongful. I will never have his kid." Maybeline said. "Okay, tell Al a divorced is in order over sexual esteem dies." He smiled. "I'm Eddie I know my weight. They don't marry me because I'm ornery." He looked at Casey and stated, "Women problems," and smiled. If she could have taken a gun and killed Eddie she would have because he mentioned sex. Casy got it none. He was thinking about the police, and what gun to use. The police department Al went out on tax invasion.

The captain of the Chicago Police Department was ten. The leas was Jack Adams. Hello police department. 1-2 make a menu view. Al Capone age twenty three should be taken out. He's frozen and we can take him out anytime. We have a court order for a state of education from the president. You wine if you take a gun in and kill him here. His signature at age ten, him on site. The note said Stage 3. It had the president's signature. The head of the state police and Al Capone's signature. The school system was on time. The year 1920's. It takes two years to get an education in the state department. You know hygiene and medical well. The time was 7:02 a.m. The police department was one trillion Chicago city police. The state police was one million.

The school trach Mrs. Sanders taught eighth grade. The state teachers hygiene and in two years you have an education. She cooked out, her hygiene was flawless. She took a bath every morning. She had a husband Bob with two kids. Bob took a bath from a well. They drew water. The two kids took one bath a week. Why try. They messed up every day. Just show them on bath days. Elain the eighth grade teacher continued if you peeved. You take it. The class was fifty and showed no emotion. You use hygiene well.

He wore a suite and a hat his choice of weapons was a thirty eight. Keep your hygiene well. He was straight Italian assassin, forty pounds overweight. Ever single soldier could take on a whole city on warfare and win against the police and all. "Did you peeve?" he asked the class. The said nothing, if you peeve your apologize. The class looked forward as Fast Eddie spoke. Peeved meant to the teach and class and Fast Eddie belched. They hygiene of the class was poor in this Chicago eighth grade 1920's. "I'm for Al Capone we support him." The Sicilian mafia build by Al Capone was one trillion death soldiers. Fast Eddie Marcum said "Is that my wife?" He spoke to his wife. "See you at the door." Eddie waved, he lost his wife that was in janitorial at the school, because he personalized her and spoke to her out could she left in two weeks when Al Capone gave permission.

The Chicago police departments were poised and ready for Al Capone. Police chief Montgomery was one of ten police chiefs born and raised in Chicago. He has then kids at age twenty three. He was married at fourteen. He work up driving the 1920's with a bath every day and coffee. His oldest daughter stated, "Kill Al Capone and get it over with." She was in high school. He drank his coffee. The .38 of Al Capone was on his hip. He smiled and touched it. "He's child's play because we have tax devoid case that is frozen to die."

Casey Thomas drank his coffee. The Italian Don hated addiction, yet he liked coffee. He looked at his wide, "Fast Eddie told the schools that we favored Al and supported him, so we can go about our business. We have over a trillion dollars in money because Al robbed all the banks in Chicago and brought back cash." Casey Marcum had over a trillion Italian assassins. They came from Chicago schools at 17. They learned weapons quick and were assigned Casey temporary. They were good at what they did and were hired to Casey for a week. "Listen, Al Capone is under indictment of the law. Kill him on sight. He has a .38 Smith and Wesson and he told carillon Michael to kill on sight. Don't ever doubt that Al Capone died at the police station and never came back. The Captain scratched his head. I want Al Capone dead.

It was midnight. The captain, Captain Marcum gave the order to move in one trillion officers. They lit their sirens blue and proceeded to Al's house for coffee cakes and death. Al Capone went to freezer units and one trillion officers converged on Al Capone. Twenty city blocks of cops. "We can't find him sir," Bill Tatum a crack officer at crim. The police coverage on Al Capone's house at midnight after ram sacking it. They proceeded back to the police state. Ten for city officers, twenty for the state cops. At 12:01 midnight, Casey gave the order from Chicago Gardens to kill the police one hundred percent the soldiers moved in and killed 1 trillion officers of the law. Casey sounded like a monkey afterwards. One hundred dead cops were around him. The mafia soldiers killed one trillion at the head Don's soldier. It was the first time ever won over the police. The reason Al Capone said he didn't want to die. It was called the Night Chicago died. Al was the biggest con of all time because he won over tax invasion. Al went to the tax office the next day. He said that he was in the wrong office by mistake. He was repaziliated for court. Eddie killed the officers, he was forty pounds overweight, and he was Fast Eddies Marcum because he was quick with firing getting it to Al Capone before the stock market closed.

The bodies of the police officers were taken out by Bull, that later became John Gott's right hand man. He resided in New York and was known to be a traitor because John Gotti went up on conspiracy charges; because his wife wasn't paid alimony. His job was to get the mafia in freezer units. He was loyal one hundred percent to Al Capone only. One trillion mafia under Bull was given a body and the bodies were incinerated. Al Capone got his money back in one minute. The court indictment was off when Fast Eddie Marcum asked the judge to parole it and he did. He has three million he stated that the officers bought weapons from. He was a black market agent. The officers bought from Germany. He owed the state one million. The tax devoid was off because he proved that he paid his taxes. History stated it took eleven years because they wanted to delay. The next day his finances were good and so were his checks. He made it through time in freezer units. He was at an airport to meet Bull was his brothers to talk about the police and rehire after the police rehire. The police went Al Capone's way none. They said, "Stay Legal and we won't arrest you." He was never arrested. He knew how to get away. An officer approached after the meeting and asked for credentials. Al looked at him, "I'm Al Capone, no ID. I'm not driving. Are you a city cop or a detailed officer?" The copy

smiled, "Airport security." He pointed, "That DC 4 airplane needs mainte-
nance what do you do?" "I don't know, I'm not a pilot. Can I go?" "No," the
airport officer stated.

Al took out a .38 and shot him. Al was the only one that knew because he
had a silencer on it. Bull picked up the bodies. "Hey Cleopatra what does
Egypt have to do with it?" Al asked running his way. Cleopatra sat mulling,
"Nothing Al Capone. Nothing." "I'll go then." Capone said. She gave him a
Jesus sticker. He said, "Thank you. You serve Jesus, I serve Jesus?" Al asked.
Al served no one. He was never taught how. Cleopatra said, "Yeah." He
laughed and ran away. Egypt was tough. Al thought light. They were one. Al
was ten in crime during the 1970's. They came after Al's money zero. That's
how they gained. Al gained because he was president with weapons.

The Hell Angels were on trillion. The Hells Angels killed anything that
ever went against them in crime. Their output was one hundred percent. Their
arrest were zero if they looked at you and said that you were dead they would
kill you if you don't correct it. Their base was Los Angeles. Their clans were
trillions. They could get in and out no one else could. They could maneuver
a bike in and out. Rumor speculated animal got into their bloodline because
they were portly and had one hundred outputs. Their deaths were one trillion
through time. They were early and ate the victim.

The Cubans were educated with equal to Greek mythology in the English
language and pronunciation of English. There were one trillion Cubans. We
went Cuba's way none because of the food thing. They eat well, then get frozen
and eat insect. The United States refused food only at the end of regency and
Cuba went to war with an underground and ended up with fruit. "Does Egypt
want anything from America would be asked when America was taken
hostage?" "No, Egypt wants nothing." Egypt did without food rarely, when
they did they were wired other countries to see if they needed food and if yes
ordered for Egypt also. The Pharaoh was honest and sincere and gained because he was bright. He compared his shaven head to anyone in the movies
fun with a shaven head and got food he paid one hundred percent.

1928 Cambodia is at war with the United States. We have a big problem.
People are angry because the president is light. We though that light meant
he was a sissy and he isn't the senate said. Let's send forces over there to equate
with Cambodia. The United States dropped down; Cambodia was one trillion
miles away and another one thousand. The commander was Stephen pastor

General of the United States Cambodia team. The United States Cambodia team lasted twenty seconds. The wild life became them. The papers said the Cambodia team lasted twenty seconds. The wild life became them. The papers said the Cambodia team failed no one came back. The soldiers ran through Cambodia trees with weapons for fifty years. The soldiers came and went. The war zones gone against were the orient one trillion dropped own and their family begged. They quit playing them. They did after two years. China came in by the trillions and was out in two weeks. They hid well. Their martial arts worked well to give them out to run and they ran and hid. They were only from Cambodia wilderness in two weeks. They were surprised they were very kind. The Hells Angels would would have lived forever because they were animalistic in all details while seemingly to carry extra weight. The next team was 1972 trade went poor. SRGT Adams stated, "National Union of Saul need reprieve", and smiled "No milk dudds. SRGT Adams flew into Cambodia in 1928 and was never seen again. We need confirmations for Milk Dudds. We never got them." SRGT Yates was confederate army. "No Milk Dudds a chewy treat we will send you more." He smiled. "The confederate army welcomes you at the end of time to serve Jesus not Satan." SRGT Adams looked out, "Milk Dudd 3 was a treat by a nation that served God. We want the president to confiscate US." "Okay yates, states we are at war with Cambodia. If you get Milk Dudds none."

"Hi I'm the president, didn't you go out on tax invasion. Let the confederate army confiscate you?" Yates replied. "Send the soldiers into Cambodia." The president stated, "We are at a state of war." "I figured you were through after." Yates replied. "That was another president. We won barely. I have money." Sent were one trillion United States military. The reason one trillion, it would take that many to cover that much space. The newspaper 1973 Journal stated: "We are still waiting for the Cambodian forces to return. Cambodian forces to return. Cambodia was trillion of miles of wilderness that stretched on forever into the jungle terrain. Cambodia has 3 waterfalls was fed by the ocean. They were ugly not pretty because Cambodia should have ended and another location started. It was the location that the United States or any military met their match and made it back none.

"How does it feel to have your private detective license and an office with a probability of solving crime?" Timmy asked. She was very pretty and sat behind his desk. Stetson smiled. "Well, I hope the clientele make it in." Stetson stated. "They will, you will do well." Timmy shook his hand by. She said, "We're family your welcome here." She left with a hug.

Egypt came in to collect when Egypt was used without permission. The Sicilian mafia when the head don Al Capone's money was taken or in jeopardy. The Middle East when stock was refused the president upon signing for stage at the state police of the president's office you had to sign or they didn't give thing up. It went off with a wave. The state police kept it forever if you're signed for something illegal like killing kids. They went off with a wave. The state police kept if forever if you signed for something illegal like killing kids. They went after you only if you had signed of illegal. .Some thought that they had police protection against organized crime. The were the same less if they came after Al and his money. The states rocked illegal none. Bull would come in hurried; he wore glasses and looked peaceful. He said that he was from Milwaukee. He asked, "Are you after Al?" He was talking about Al Capone crime syndicate. Bull was from Chicago. "Don't be after him," he said, "He's for you." He smiled and said, "Go after him none. He's nice." They would say why they were after him and the mafia would come in and kill, then if they wanted Al Capone dead. He would shoot them in the head and run. He looked civilized. He was very organized at crime on John Gotti. He turned only seventy; get him back to freezer units. Egypt collected on Egypt. They would come in with a gun and kill if you spoke badly about the head pharaoh. The Egyptians won if you qualified Egypt one hundred percent. They were the most successful because Egypt knew their spectrum.

John Gotti crime syndicate 3 meant he went out on tax invasion. If asked the Don, John Gotti state no, He was crime syndicate. New York mean to be ran crime in New York. He was an ace at crime. His incarceration was your wife want money. Here's money, he gave her a hundred dollars. Her name was Linda. The judge stated protocol off signed. This wave's okay John Gotti signed. This is John Gotti protocol off please. He signed his name and stated keep it off. He killed Linda with a .44 Smith and Wesson to play any government game you signed John Gotti was married to her three weeks. John Gotti's death was announced on the news.

Al Capone's brother, John Gotti was alive. He ran organized crime in New York. He was good at it. He was exceptional to the mafia which meant he kept crime out of New York. That went against the mafia. John Gotti was successful one hundred percent. His Italian soldiers numbered one trillion; he was successful because Al Capone backed him only. He had a strategic mind for crime.

The year was 1972, I John Gotti. I have New York, I work for Al Capone. He's still alive. His assets were two house and one million dollars His wife Santa Fe came late. His IQ was high. He made money easily and sent it through Al Capone and Al sent him back what was his. Case Marcum was Los Angeles. He had two houses one in Los Angeles flood zone; sandtraps meant you sent feet below. The ocean and at much kens fate meant stewed tomatoes or rice cakes, people liked that. They were safe. It was like a trap door against the ocean. Casey went to freezer units not sane traps. He liked Los Angeles because Al Capone sent him.

John Gotti was a Louisville Don that sank gourmet coffee into trillion dollar businesses; because he sank L.A. with gourmet coffee during 1980. The coffee was loaded in caffeine and the seas were high. He dealt drugs and ran a mafia of one trillion Sicilian. 1922, the room was full of Sicilian mafia soldiers. John Gotti was Al Capone's brother. He announced John to a room full of Italian soldiers. He's your boss. Al was straight Italian. He did not sound like a monster, a beast or a freak. He was very high in charisma as much as 1980 character Sylvester Stallone or Bruce Willis. Al Capone announced John Gotti. He was exceptional of the wills, meant he brought Al's money back John Gotti said I accept and said, "You're my brother." Al said, "You're my brother, you reside in Louisville Kentucky." John Gotti's record was high for the mafia.

The Egyptian pharaoh that heads the Egyptians was in his office in Egypt. The Egyptian record was one hundred percent. They were from the Middle East and had high output. "Uh oh. Al Capone went out on tax invasion. Let's get frozen, the Italians are evil on losses of money. He sold guns to the Middles East henceforth he had weapons and could kill." The Egyptians one trillion, one trillion times were frozen for 28 years. Al Capone age twenty three received his money in one week. His organization was a killer Sicilian army. The sign they left was none. The mafia was one trillion, one thousands times of a Sicilian army. They won because they were good at warfare. The Hells Angels were one trillion, one thousand times. The were evil again anything that went against them. The confederate army was one trillion, trillions of times. Any enemy that they conquered could receive the mark of the beast and join the army died Embalmed and judged guilty and sent to Hell. The person that joined was killed and revealed confederacy. The leader Jed Clampit went out on tax invasion. The confederacy would attack at the end of time. Takeover they won, or were taught to wine. They were documented during the Civil War 1800's.

Tim Mathews was Cuban born; he was educated to speak English appropriately well. He went to school in New Jersey Central Heights. Tim's goods were good. There were one trillion Cubans the same, their persona. The Cubans were very friendly. Their output and friendliness was equivalency to a Hispanic born American, which was extremely nice if asked the difference. Time Mathews would say that he was Cuban and he was Hispanic. He has nothing to do with Cuba. They were themselves. They would go to war for a roomful of fruit. All they had to say was they wanted real food and they would be presented a voucher by the president for free food. Just state you are here for the state department religion and all they feed the hungry. They go to war with the communist way of life and know nothing of the Middle East of warfare Egypt is what I will be. I will be the biggest pharaoh of time. Communism will be my way of life. Tim stated at twenty three. He was a college educated and knew that he would run Egypt. The robes of the Middle East would belong to the Egyptian though the stature and height of the Cuban male was 5'5". Tim and his one trillion Cubans would mate and inhabit Egypt in the Middle East as Cubans with shaven heads through freezer units and out on a four. The Rabbis of the Middle East was educated in the United Sates. Their appearance and manners were good. The collected and won on Egypt, being used they had titles and won.

When Egypt was used without permission the Egyptians presented a good case. Egypt was determined different and with priest of a Middle Eastern communist country. They won one hundred percent when the pharaoh's life was in danger. The women had kids and were trained to be evil and go against America only when when they stated the United States was more powerful than the Middle East. They Egyptians called it the John Wayne Syndrome. That meant that the Middle East wanted food and would buy when the United States trade representative brought up warfare and religion of the Middle East. It was like going against a country that was friendly and would buy and pay one hundred and causing disagreement over the Middle Eastern ways and customs. The Middle Eastern countries trained warfare. They knew no difference and spent most of their time and money on weapons. Trade would be clear, the food dispensed to the Middle East bought and warfare was none. If the trade representative was rude the foreign country did not understand as a Cuban original that was the highest leadership of Egypt. Those who suspected that Egypt was Cuban devil were none, most thought that Egypt was a new generation.

Stetson looked into cases. He was impressive with computer programmability. He was trained military now detective agency. He asked the programmer to run Nation Geographic worlds and city access through. She liked him, a complied that he could get in and out of locations of city and country, and state unscathed. They could enter into any location with car and access to his money as a detective he would be able to access all sides of a situation and all angles. Stetson was a good looking man in his prime. He used systems to his advantage in computers. The main idea was to not get in trouble with uniformed police officers and to remain exempt none if though of well in a legal country security is supposed to go to treatment. Security upon being called should speak to security or security is the police department. If counselors were legal and the head department, the police went their own way in institute and state hoopsters. If charged and state institute were charged and they didn't change things they went to people and harmed of affected on hundred percent upon the institute being illegal.

Stetson processed computers to have output on the job in and out. Systems of computers were instituted through time freezer units and when issued or invented was a question what countries through warfare's. Inventors and programmers, that countries would want to live through warfare placed in a computers and your vitals. If you came out a four that was you in a double body you maintained your life and stayed young and some lived through wars. You gained if one hundred percent frozen if someone brought you through time and out of freezer units. The FBI would double for people in freezer units if they came against the president in crime.

Cases came and went for Stetson. He was actually well defined at private detective work. Stetson gained a good reputation at his job. He solved some cases of jewelry missing, foreign was an area that Stetson was well rehearsed in detective a five line in crime when it fell down and the chips were counted out. He was legal. The series of Colombo aired late, late at night. The actor that played Colombo was Don Johnson featured in Miami Vice as a series that aired during the 80's was Don Johnson who played a narcotic officer in Miami Florida. Sonny Crocket was a Miami Vice squad that assorted drug trade.

TUBBS was his partner. The original actor in Colombo was Peter Falk who played the lieutenant of a police force. The series aired during the 70's. Peter Falk was the first Colombo on the series. Don Johnson played from 1:30 duck to 7:11 dawn. People slept as someone fevered turned on Colombia and Don who signed on to play Deputy Harry. The second to Clint Eastwood the movie were incorporated by a company that was expensive that took the most popular actor of the 1980's and through time they registered high the most because time changed. Activing differently and the company reincorporated the style in the present day output and recast the present a style that lost in present to the 80's today. Remake of detectives, guns and styles.

Don Johnson went from Colombo to Dallas. He played Dirty Harry. Colombo went into a series. Bruce Willis plated in another couple of movies from the untouchables, he played Al Capone crime syndicate of Chicago. Tom Hanks played Elliott Ness, people that played Bruce Willis were edited in to keep the style of the movies alive. The actors were paid. Tom Cruise played Elliott Ness first, second Tom Hanks. Tom Arnold played the sheriff in the Heat of the Night, original was Carol O'Connor reedited. It was a show in for Carol O'Connor a reproduction of All in the Family, Married with Children with Al Bundy. Rosie a comedy with Rosanne Barr, Archie Bunker a fictional character, Al Bundy played his brother. The actors were matched the same age with Rosie, a sister, the three were brothers and the sister was Rosie. The comedy was remade in actors' ages for age and combined comedy.

Stetson's cases were steady. He was clever at getting into locations and extracting facts. Stetson took on cases and solved them. He took on cases of school teachers, ministers and most anyone that needed a case solved. He was charismatic and very good at his work. "Hi, I'm Lisa Baker." "Hi, Stetson is my name. I am here as a private detective from the United States. I was straight passenger to and from the United States. I want to trade on your company. Please make certain I make it back please." "Okay, we will send you back." Lisa stated. "What can I help you with?" Stetson's office in England was very polished, very comfortable, very traditional, the seats behind and in front of Lisa's desk were very comfortable. The portraits on the wall were very distinguished of England a country that bought product from America and was alias one hundred percent. They went America's way ninety eight percent when they didn't was when they did not dispense product.

Lisa smiled, "I need help with Egypt, and I have a clothing line at Bakers Department Store, a department store here in London. We are very tradition and Bakers is an older business that we Bakers have distributed clothing through time. Egypt claimed on Egyptians line of clothing stating permission was not granted, and they would like the money earned and the Egyptian line of clothing and jewelry shut down. The Egyptians win most of the time when they go after the Egyptian name being used." "Was the line of clothing distributed from Egypt and the jewelry?" "No, it was patented after Egypt from after the United States. The jewelry was the United States. It states international both were export/import." Stetson was reassuring.

"The Egyptians are good at collections." "President Byers in responsible for exports/imports." She was distinguished and pretty. Her makeup was smart, she laughed she looked like a chicken. Stetson cackled "President Byers." They both laughed. She stated, "He who was held hostage by a pretty Caribbean girl." They laughed for five minutes over President Byers who was tied down with ropes. By an AAA Paradise Island woman and missed out on trade meeting that were important to the United States on foreign trade. Lisa Baker looked coy and pretty, her cackle and laughs over. "I apologize Stetson, I know that we are allies to America. Are you surprised with exports/imports and the presidency?" "I too laughed." Stetson reminded. "I have a partner for you. He's very good at being a spy. He was popular in British intelligence and was known in the movie business. England is an old country and he was a favorite at countering the enemy. We are allies with America and he's no enemy to America. He was frozen through time and was excellent at detail. Stetson I would like for you to meet your partner, James Bond."

"Hi, I'm James Bond." "James were an expensive suit and was immaculate at grooming. His eyes were brown. He looked like a cousin to Pierce Bronson. He was good looking. "Hi, I'm Stetson." He shook James Bond's hand. Stetson smiled. "It's nice to meet you, I knew of your existence none except in the movies and books. "It's a pleasure." Bond was very charming, a man of forty. His charisma was high. Stetson liked him with charisma such as James' had. You had to be paid a lot of money.

'She updated me on the Egyptians usually we English just say the English are English and the Egyptians, Egyptians give the Egyptians what's theirs and they are happy. The Egyptians win highly because they know how to take money." Bond and Stetson had an expensive lunch and went to James Bond and went over the details. The state department paid for lunch. The two went made a game plan and went to James Bond's office. "How many people if I may ask and I'm only curious made it through time such as you James?" Stetson inquired. James was behind his desk. "They were about ten. Al Capone was one, Tony Montana a Cuban drug dealer would be another if he would have went into freezer units." "Do you gain credit for your profession?" James asked. "Yes, you will be paid Stetson and accredited." James stated.

James had a universal computer that linked. He went over Stetson's record. He saw that his wife was killed by Cuba. James had dark eyes, he looked at Stetson concerned upon the point out of his wife's death. He looked at him, "You have military experience, import/export." James reminded. "Yes." Stetson stated, "As Baker knew. Since she hired me. I was proud as punch that she knew my record" Stetson smiled. Bond smiled. "The John Wayne Syndrome." "I know the foreign exchange rule that warfare was confused with religion. Egypt rates high on output when the pharaoh states clam on Egypt they are as powerful as your Sicilian Mafia and were around longer. They are dangerous. Some Americans really never saw the Middle East up close. The Egyptians are old and traditional. Their military is good." James stated. "It's not a lot in titles if Baker had titles for dispensing Egyptian clothing." Stetson stated.

"I know that Egypt is finally about who they give claim to use. They are very high in criminal law and have a military of one trillion. They win because they have output to claim on anything used on the country Egypt." Bond knew the Middle East one hundred percent. They were angry only if or mostly when stock was refused or they would not accept stock back when unhappy. Bond was flamboyant and had high output as a spy. He was educated high as way Egypt. The pharaohs and one hundred percent of Egypt were educated high.

The president held meetings and kept the white house up. Society was unaware of the hostage situations that only lasted a couple of days. It was difficult to imagine a country or a president holding his own country hostage with a country such as Cuba. President Byers was groomed well with the presidential style for suits. President Byers spoke well of the military and the state of the nations. "Bond James Bond is this the Egyptian state department? You have reached Egypt Mr. Bond who would you like to speak with?" "The head department of grants and right and patrons of an commercialized and commercialization." "What are the commercialization Mr. Bond? If its Egypt we commercialize our own country." James Bond is known to be a state department legalized spy your titles are in order. James was dressed in a suit that accentuated him. He looked like a good looking cousin to Pierce Bronson. He clicked a pin on the deck he had it for writing. He was practical on his output on British time. If the queen was spoken of unfavorably he said bye and asked for another worker in that case. His suit was smart not peacock, yet most were practical. Even in arrogance dress and had output in areas of the state department.

"Much like England the Egyptians state department stated we commercialized ourselves, our military collect upon our advancement being disrespected. If you have a signature and permission you know it if not know publishers and book forms are fiction and most know that and gain a like it as a compliment. Most want to be known in the movies on their merits as long as the men were men and the women were women." The prosecutor laughed. He stated, "I not want to be known to wear panty hose yet my wife looked good in them." Bond winced. "No one wants to be known as male lingerie being female. "Boxers." The representative stated, "White." Ron stated. Regular for men."

Bond returned the topic, "Does Baker Department of England has permission to sell Egyptian clothing?" The Egyptian representative was brown like a cigar. He was in the sun. The Egyptians original race was Cuba, no one knew that. "Not a chance." "Can we buy rights or run clothing through?" "No." "Did you know of Bakers Clothing Store?" "Yes, no Egyptians. Thanks Mr. Bond." "Change it." "James stated to Mr. Baker. 'Egypt is very particular. Their military is fierce and Egypt is being used. No permission." Baker looked over the papers with the Egyptian state department and stamped on.

She got on the food to her head of management department. "Hi Lewie. Pull the Egyptian department and fill it." "Yes Mrs. Baker." Bakers Department file Egypt and gave the pharaohs the profits. The store continued making money. Stetson was at Bond's office waiting for Bond's report. Bond came in the case is complete you receive payment for plane fare and cost. Bond updated him and Stetson flew back and opened his office door. He picked up his mail up from his receiving box. Stetson flew back and opened his office door. His picked his mail up from his receiving box. Stetson ran warfare through his computer A to Z. All locations played from A to Z from the confederacy to the Gulf War to any war the United States and foreign fought. Stetson had a very collective mind and was bright at warfare. Stetson had an equal to the world or house he had in the movies. Security cameras brought the enemy out in computer dynamics the computer enhanced the intruder circled and held the image if a break in the police were called automatically. Stetson slept in a basement and solved cases. He woke up to coffee and conversation with his secretary. His IQ was high, he was capable of support through his private detective agency and he paid him secretary and had food. He also paid his programmer and for expensive computer. He bought a program block from expensive companies that wanted to sell such as IBM; Apple 2 etc the systems were expensive.

Jed Clampit signed that he would like to have his story told. The Milwaukee born oil well man was in a comedy that aired and was very funny. The actor was a spitting image of Jed Campit who later plated in Barnaby Jones.. The series aired a long time. "Hi I'm Hed and I'm in the oil well business. Granny is my mother. I listen to her, I have sex with me not her." The Milwaukee born oil man wore a big brown hat that reminded people of a hillbilly. "You will be popular in the oil business just don't go against your mom." The state department was a pretty Italian with brown hair. Linda was tax department she was the head of the tax department and stated that his hat fit him. Jed was a sixty eight year old man. His mom was ninety. She had Jed at a Milwaukee Hospital. Her granny was Clementine because she was a Cleomous from New York. Jed was highly influential in the oil business and lost money seldom.

Jed had three barns outside the country. One in New York, one in New Orleans, and on in Albany Kentucky He thought that they were hillbilly and he was not. He was a Milwaukee Brewster. He was southern more than northern in his ways. He went out and three of his prized pigs had ribbons. He pulled them off and killed one of them for meat. It bred and ruined most of the meat way sorry and was listed under real meat. Real meat had to be processed without parasites. "My prized pig was killed, I shot it." Granny was college educated. "You know that soy has no parasite yet turns to pudding the second time you eat it because it's designed to taste like real meat. Jed presented the three ribbons, red, blue, and white. I took these from the girls school The ribbons had hair in them where he took them off the pigs. Granny believe that he acquired them in school. Jed goes to the tax department and we will see if you're legal. Those girls had a right to live she was talking about girls in Jed's third grade class. Jed went to the tax office and lost on tax invasion and would never gain in the United States for Jed Clampit it was the worst. It was like giving your spirit to someone else and everything you had whose doggy the tax department asked. The Milwaukee born Jed Clampit what that meant. "I meant." Jed stated, "Someone ran over my dog." He smiled two minutes. Later he lost on tax invasion. It meant you speak well to neighbors or they come in with the police. Whose doggy means you behave well of they kill your dog you smile and says who doggy. I lost my doggy here's a dollar don't kill my wife." Jed laughed, "If you have a bad report with neighbors they could kill you insensitive. By not liking you and calling the police every ten minutes. In the summer Jed wore his hillbilly hat. I like to be treated well. Jethro was Jethro Marcum, he was Jed's right hand man in oil.

The reason they called him Boa Deane was he made it to a business meeting and he stated, "I'm bovine you're bovine from Kentucky." Jed Clampit gets rid of that hat or I'll call you a Kentucky souse that ate bovine sandwiches. I'm a bovine if your don't take that stupid hat off. Jethro's education was college administration. Jed smiled. "They were two hundred businesses in oil at present." "Okay." Jed stated with a smile. "You're Jethro bovine?" Jethro smiled okay that's me. He showed up with a straw hat and a rope tied around his pants. A rope for holding hay bells. It was golden. He showed up twice a week. "Okay bovine your Jethro Bovine." "I am but I want off the hook." Jethro stated. "No, your bovine and I wear the hat." Jed stated. "Okay." Jethro stated. He was bovine for one week. Jed wore the hat forever more. Jed was the president or leader of the confederacy an original organization that attempted to take over in the 1880's, however it worked out he went out on tax invasion and would never earn. He was violent and moved to the south after being completely ruined. His mom moved with him to Birmingham Alabama along with his right hand man Jethro and his daughter Elly Mae. All were in the series, the Beverly Hillbillies. Jed was walking dead man that hated everything and would go in with a shotgun and kill everything man, woman or child because he went out on tax invasion and they tried selling him religion.

Jed would build a confederacy of one trillion one trillion times enough to repopulate America for however long and bring them back. They were a dark army that was unknown to live past the 1880's. The devil could with kill everybody in America and ruin time, even end it. The generals were twenty three, embalmed and brought back from hell in Satan's name if killed the army would come back recreated from hell. They wore beards and wigs only for the 1800's, when Abraham Lincoln was determined dead. General Grant shot him, he moved in next to Abraham Lincoln looking like a fat slob. He wore pillows and spoke with a hearing deficiency. He mom was straight A Italian and known to be Daniels, a family that made it through time. They were two million. They were build AAA and won mend with grace. He was dead and embalmed. She was in twenty years, the Daniels cal went her way that she was dead, left of the family was two million.

Jesse James was of that clan and shared the same mother as General Grant. He was as big a killer as General Grant. Jesse James confederacy killed Billy the Kid's family because William Bonnie said he served Satan upon going to freezer units. Jesse looked at Billy and said, "Your family dead or alive?" William Bonnie said, "Dead, there is only two alive." Jesse shot them. Kids and all. There were two million, his dad was sheriff and William Bonnie had two kids, nineteen and twenty. "What he said was wrong, kill them at last." He said, "No, let them live." He wanted them alive. Jesse James was dead and brought back Satan. His boss Jed Clampit went out on tax invasion. William Bonnie thought that they were friends. He turned money back in to the government and picked up government grants. He killed two million state cops because his mom was beaten. They were involved in saying innocent to his dad on wife beaten. The last thing they said was, "Billy you were family." Billy smiled and said, "My mom was beaten." Pat Garrett said were family and let him go. If arrested hid dad would have got him out. His dad William Bonnie serious was a crack as state marshal. The person he beat his wife so Billy would grow up straight Italian and not a sissy. The confederacy picked up the availability to freeze themselves for worlds that ended. Jed was a crack at living through time.

Williams Bonnie came out of the freezer units in 1978. He smiled and said, "Who runs crime?" Al Capone stated he did. William Bonnie said, "I would like to join you." Al Capone who already hired and incorporated his Sicilian killers and Don of the biggest killers stated; "We don't need any Irish looking Italians." If William Bonnie would have blinked he would have been dead. "I'll be on your side." Al took the safety off the .38, Billy shook his hand and said, "We will be friends." "Friends." Al said. Jesse James said "I'll kill you only at the end of time." Al shot him. He was recreated instantly. Al regretted that he didn't shoot him time and time again. He could have been shot one million times and been recreated. Al put a gun to Billy's head and said, "Are you against me?" "No." William Bonnie said, "I will never be against you." Al Capone left with high endurance.

Jesse said I killed your family Billy. You were light picking up state funding and killing state sheriffs. You will go to hell and we will embalm you. Billy was seasoned and swore and took off. Jed Clampit was on a level 2, a computer generated leave no one could see you. You could wave your hand through them and they would laugh. He wore a trench coat and jeans. He had a shot gun. "Billy don't be a hero, come back and make me your wife." Billy done be a hero was released in two weeks. Jed signed, William Bonnie under Pet Talspon. The song was about Jesse James killing William Bonnie's family. It went number one for one year. Billy crossed his fingers and said, "I hope they're alive, if not they died of old age in the 1800's either way they were dead," Billy carried a .38. He said I guess it was for AL. A .38 was a powerful handgun. He bothered Al none in time.

In 1978 John Gotti took crime in New York, he was Al Capone's brother. Casey Marcum was Ney York. John Gotti Louisville, Al was brothers. They were ten brothers of the Capone Sicilian crime family. Each had one trillion soldiers that protected the Don's assets. Bull was a brother he was known to take on John Gotti in New York when actually he incarcerated John Gotti back to freezer units. They bragged about crime none. It was like asking for penitentiary time. No one knew their output. Their boss Al thought well on a graduate of college into business of crime. He knew how to perform against a state department that wanted him dead with weapons. His signature of stage three at ten was forgotten. He was a good kid at ten and could not believe his mother had him sign at the state police office. The state moved his class, processed him He didn't know why at twenty three. The president said stage one and the state police were ready to move in because as a young boy of ten his mom said sign. "Okay mom." He signed and he didn't know what it was. You were suppose to know what it was or it went off for stage 3 and the Chicago police department.

Stetson work up in his basement location. He collected some calls on his video answering machine. He addressed people well on bond. He was acknowledged in affairs of the Middle East and tied things up well or settled them. Stetson knew his past. He was expensive on cases. Bond was startling and lived up to his name. Stetson had coffee in a basement near his office that showed up in time none. The Cubans were originally Egyptians. Those under that ruling were evil by the trillions. They modified education from the United States high weather though England of depiction of time. They looked shaven or some had hair over a trillion on thousand times. They looked like the head pharaoh on the Ten Commandments. He was Cuban an original. Jed was modified from the 1800's confederacy to be a through time.

Stetson worked programs through on warfare, a detective that went into his field and got him, in and out of clients. He had programs for real estate. He utilized the output in computer technology and paid for computer stores A to Z. It helped enhance his field and got him, in and out of clients. He had programs for real estate. He utilized the output in computer technology and paid for computer stores A to Z. It helped enhance his field of detective. Dirty Harry Callahan was trained on the Los Angeles police department. Uniformed police training. Harry was twenty five and out of training and into a uniform for LAPD. His Captain was Tim Black. His uniform detail was parades and sleaze bars. He hated parades were scheduled by the state department. Some parades had light shows. The colors were florescent, it was uncanning in a college commercial. White, aqua, red did with also blue and computerized Halloween. Here orange with environment that the computer ordered, cotton candy was sweet along with carnival pop corn and candy apples with peanuts. The fireworks show was a color that was brilliant. The star filled sky had no clouds in it. The universal paramount movie parade took sheets of Los Angeles by storm. The movie business was a lucrative business and entertainment with a good dose of commercialization prompted a colorful event that started with art museums. The cops made it congested or smooth with floats, clowns, bands and litter patrol. People usually liked parades. Harry Callahan was one of hundreds that patrolled parades and sleaze bars. The police looked for the parades starting on time and ending on time. They looked for illegals. If found they prosecuted and got them out somehow. Harry was one of millions of cops in Los Angeles. Los Angeles was known to be the movie capital for Central America. It was a city that America dreamed about. It was shown with palm trees and wondrous locations. The series came out for TV. The news and the awards were aired. Cable brought in a lot. It helped if you scheduled programs, the sports enthusiast enjoyed their games. Portrait studios emerged. It was city that thrived well, work relations were high.

Harry was trained fully as a uniformed police office. His job was a regular eight hour shift. He was assigned and completed his job thoroughly. The cops of Los Angeles were very smart. Los Angele's crime was controlled by Casey Marcum. He was Al Capone's brother who during the 1920's dropped a police department that wanted Al dead. Casey Marcum ran lounger equal with or with permission granted from the state play boy clubs. Equal to prostitution. He ran Hustler, an exotic tanning oil Hawaiian tropic club, Independent déjà vu and AAA Exotic Adult Entertainment. He was straight Italian and had one trillion soldiers of Sicilian. Most in the United States did not know that he was alive. The dark shadows of the Sicilian Mafia was registered crime. As the reputations pronounced and picked up on the Sicilian Mafia. The Sicilian Don kept up with the finances well. Customers paid and were bothered none. The organization that racketeered over a trillion soldiers.

The Don, Casey Marcum was capable of anything crime related. They checked things out and had a record of one hundred percent accuracy to who the enemy was. They killed as hit men only when the Don was in danger. The mafia was accredited for any form of crime and would surprise you of drug deals and money laundering. They stayed away from child molestation or killing kids because kid were not involved. The XXX Adult Entertainment brought in a lot of money for the Don Casey Marcum who sent it to Al in Chicago. The head Don and founder of the Mafia. The mafia liked cops none because they affiliated none. They killed them only when they tried to overtake Don in business or kill him. The mafia won one hundred percent in any gun battle with the cops because they were experienced with guns beyond belief. They were experienced with guns beyond belief. They were real tough.

Harry was prudent. The Los Angeles police department was strict. Harry checked out parades. He was detailed strip clubs, Casey Marcum met him. He was known by the police none. He was back in his office. "Just making my rounds." Harry stated. He was wearing a uniform. If an officer came into a business he usually had a reason. You were clear and legal yet he could find a flaw then or tomorrow according to the day. Casey was the worst business man to find the mafia ran none. They were backed by Al Capone one hundred percent. It was the only locations throughout time that an officer of the law lost. The Sicilians of the mafia had a reputation. They held it on crime. The body was taken care of the mafia was one hundred percent certain. They wanted them dead. John Gotti was bogus. His wife signed for stage 2 and was pressured by the police. "I was assigned to the strip clubs. Is everything ok?" Harry stood 6'2". He had brown hair, a uniform and gun. He was smart and very good with weapons. "I don't need the police go." Casey said, "If they said okay and went they gained if not they were shot in the head." "If you need me call."

Harry got into his patrol car and left. There were no disturbances. Harry developed a sense for survival along the way. The mafia were not animals, however they were excellent with weapons and thought well because they were educated and knew detail well. The organizations was very street wise and fought well. They knew their area well.

If the police got a line on the mafia after the 1920's they would have sent them straight into he penitentiary for a lifetime. Harry Callahan's report was no disturbances. "John Gotti died three times since the 1920's. He had a funeral and returned to work the next day." He went by the name John Gotti. His men worked for him on hundred percent if Al said too if Al said no he was high in output on crime. He was considered too extravagant of the wills of Capone organized crime. He was good at everything. He sold drugs and everything. He had then kids, his mafia was one trillion soldiers.

The Los Angeles officers helped in areas that didn't show up to the average American citizen. By schedule on parades, making certain it was safe in and out, the police tried to minimal illegal by prosecution of drugs and drunken drivers. The checked the Triple X clubs out when asked on legal, the cops educated when scheduled in local areas. Their main concern was keeping Los Angeles legal. The LAPD was big. Harry Callahan ticked one day, he went on calls absorbed drugs, when called the police checked and illegal Harry worked as a uniformed police officer for ten years. Harry was raised in a location that was controlled by criminal law. The United States citizen was accounted for by the state department of the US from the school system to the city and state police to go to school from kindergarten to first grade to graduate 12 if their job qualified it College t\and into the work related world. Harry was raised around criminals. They cross matched themselves to the parents and family for a whole neighborhood. How crime worked was they looked like the citizens and became them. They held them hostage or detained them during the process. The crime as animalistic and won one hundred percent of the time. They got away from the cops one hundred percent on a Harley Davidson. Folklore spoke of werewolves, there were vampires depicted. The Twilight Zone went from black and white a serious on TV into color and into a movie. The actual hoore spoke weird about weird about Linda Blare. It spoke of religion in ultimate usually the state moved in in some ways such as bizarre behavior yet movies were listed as entertainment not religion.

The police usually modified unusual in and processed it legal. They knew no better. Harry's dad was high in IQ and got freezer units so that he could like his life out with his wife. Freezer units were how packaged by the state. Early in the 1900's if the state department froze you on a level B you were somehow an enemy of the state and came back none. The president replaced you with the FBI. Harry's dad was college educated, he needed his education fully to liv his life out. His name was Tim Callahan, his wife Lisa was research scientist. She was a crack at dispensing Bull He liked her because she was pretty and got along with her colleagues well. The crime was a recreation of beast that were recreated by mistake for eternity and placed back. The organization made it through time from Saddam and Gomorrah. Humans lived they were Cobras that named themselves. The Hells Angels. The lost city of Havana was a location that venomous life was increased in time by a DNA that Bill Richards developed from steroids. These built up your body twenty two percent with protein. It lasted one day. Bill was college educated and determined to be a genius because he designed programs that worked. The DNA lasted one minute or forever according to whether you looked for a solution or not. Bill Richard intravenously shot drugs to absorb the pain. He grew two inches. His physique grew one hundred percent. He worked out in the country near the state parks the spider population was high he had a cure for the venom. Ten of the research scientist he was big for two weeks. The antidote worked in seconds and he went back to his own size. Bill thru the empty syringe into a trash dumpster with candy apples and female hygiene and male from toilet being out.

The state park of Havana was two miles school was in. The animal kingdom came in and ate. The tarantulas from the zoos grew one hundred percent The Eagle grew, spiders grew, and venomous snakes. The state police were called, one million. The police sprayed the animal community died in trillion they mated and had trillions. It was a jungle out in farmlands. The woods were fifty miles was black widow tarantulas. They killed in one bite and ate the bodies. The DNA caused them to be big. The police sprayed and they died. They were professional. A black widow tarantula devil in webs took on his last victim, Ray Johnson a black professor from Havana. Sebastian held the venomous animals of Havana in a computer and reentered them after the police left. He released them and took over Havana slowly. Fifty miles of Havana's farmland was infected by animals. They killed the farmers and became them. Havana went on for years.

The Hells Angels lived from Saddam and Gomorrah. They built tunnels into the city of Los Angeles. The organization was law over police, schools, or any department. Harry Callahan was raised under the Hells Angels law more than the state and city police. He knew of crime and had a good ear for it. He lost his dad at an old age and his mom was older. His dad added life by carious against bikers. Harry Callahan worked the uniformed cop schedule for at least ten years. The situations were high. The tickets were high, the arrest were high. They were lots of court appearances. He was strict his hair was cut police short. His uniform was clean. He checked organizations out from top to bottom. There were millions of cops just like Harry across the country. They were smart and knew how to get you from here to there. The police siren went off. The car pulled over. Harry looked in the back and the front of the car. "Are you moving?" Callahan pulled over. Harry looked in the back and front of the care. "Are you moving?" Callahan asked. "Yes officer. I'm moving." The driver of the car smiled nervously. "What did I do wrong?" "You were speeding; let's see your diverse license." His name was Jake Brewster. Harry checked him out and checked the merchandise out. He knew it was stolen. "You are under arrest." "I know the commissioner, come on lets go." "Haven't you done anything illegal? Let me go."

Harry placed him under arrest and processed him. Jake went before the judge to let him off. The just said you can go. Harry hated it, yet Jake went. He was free of all charges. Jake left quickly his organization was not known because they were not processed in the state. He would fill the streets of Los Angeles with drugs and incorporate crime in Harry's honor. Harry would re-mark you were speeding. Officers knew crime twenty eight percent what they didn't know was if some are called in a crime you check their credentials out to see if they were legal or illegal. Jake Brewster was the next generation of the Hells Angels. The first generation knew Harry's record and was raised around his family. They knew his record well enough to his nervous system on resolve and take him to zero on a family incentive. There were trillions of the next generation and they were mean and animalistic. Their dens of Hells Angels were all over Los Angeles.

Harry was in plain clothes at a convenient store carrying a six pack of coke upon two of Jake's men set strategy with weapons to robe because Harry arrested their boss. They carried .38's, "Okay this is a robbery." The had ski mask on, "This makes me look bad as a drug dealer." Stephen Foster was 19, he was black and of straight streets. "Let me or our gang Ajax will be at war with you." The black man of nineteen ran drugs high. He profited with a silver Mercedes and loaded with features. Two of Stephen Foster's men moved in. Stephen was popular off the street as head of a drug dealer organization that was prudent at protection. Two of Stephen Foster's men went in with guns. The Hells Angel's fired three men were killed of Ajax. The Hells Angels pointed the gun at the cashier, "Empty it. Do you have the combination to that bank that you drop money in when you exceed the mark?"

Steve Watson worked for the convenience store three months. The blood of drug dealers smeared the walls you could tell three blacks were dead. Harry maneuvered a pistols from one of the drug dealers that had been shot. The money was handed over. Harry was still. Once of the Hells Angels lifted his gun, Harry fired at him. The bullet hit him in the head. The others was shot both were dead there were five deaths. The police arrived and Harry gave his story and was found innocent and kept his job. He passed on being in the papers and returned to work in uniform. The next day the five were listed under their organization of three drug dealers slain and two Hells Angels by off duty cop. Harry hated the situation highly. The captain looked at Harry and said, "You are FBI your orders are to protect the people not the president." Harry smiled, "You got it." Harry's move was to Chicago Illinois. He reported in to the captain. He went through training and became an FBI agent. He was trained well, his police uniform was filed away. His typical attire was suit that was brown or blue with a tie. He went to his office, the location was in Illinois. The street was Gotham. Gotham Illinois had ten levels that we ten down and complete cities of Illinois. You got there by special computers and excised on level present. Level none, the police found them none. The organization came from BTOA looking like anything but themselves. The chances of incarceration was zero. They hit of became an aspect of this world in seconds. The only chance of arrest was to catch them during process of crime and prosecute them on level A, present level.

Dirt Harry had a license threw law enforcement. The federal bureau of investigation. He was trained in law enforcement, he knew how to behave and have a high output in criminal law. He carried a holster gun and had a whole department to absorb and incarcerate crime. He was going into a beehive of bees that stung crime, was his in Illinois. The Chicago district. "Good morning, Harry, you are out on the street make certain that you are on top of criminal law. You carry a .44. It's the most powerful hand gun ever made. Use it against the enemy not friends. Arrest them you have a badge the FBI backs you. Don't go against anyone legal and we will pay you. Your girlfriends say your kinky and don't be and they will like you." The captain of the FBI stated.

Harry looked around the room without expression like the captain was a bug. He wore a brown suite with a tie. His shoes were dress his hair had grown more through FBI training. His hair was brown and slightly curly. His stature was 6'2". "I'm not kinky captain." "You're not; I thought that you liked to be tied down?" The captain Tim Matthews looked scolding Harry smiled, "No." "Okay your Harry arrest some today and keep your license." "Okay." Harry said. His badge was on his side pocked, "You're the boss." Tim smiled, "Get out of here." "Captain" Harry ran out with no charges which was impossible with the captain. "He was real good looking and masculine. I wonder what he looked like in a uniform. Get me a picture." His secretary Sandy was very pretty she handed him a picture of Harry in uniform. He looked like the other officers no different. The Joker did hard crime. His metabolism was different. His crimes were hardcore he was arrested for armed robbery; the Exxon penitentiary was bizarre for him because it closed everyone was moved. The state pen was located in the middle of an island that the ocean engulfed. Air travel was only way out. Joker was in a location called 2 ½. It was a room on ½ level that dishes were stored for the kitchen. He was an employee of the kitchen. Joker was asleep and within twenty eight minutes every body was being moved He was called Butcher Timerson, the name fit because he was strict. He woke Joker up and took him to his cell. He hit him three times with his billy club. Joker reflexed from the pain and shot Butcher in the neck and breaking it. Joker had Butcher's gun, Butcher slid out and closed the door. "You will do a lot of time over this Joker." Butcher slid down the hall, he couldn't sit up because his neck was broken. Joker pointed the gun and squeezed the trigger. Butcher died. The pistol had only on bullet in it because Butcher loaded only one when the warden called for the guards

Joker was locked in the cell. The pen was empty. His only hopes of leaving was the dead guard that he shot. He was locked down tight. Exxon was forgotten. The ocean boomed and roared. It was black and crashed on the penitentiary sometimes it flooded light and the ocean regressed. Joker was without food he would have died of starvation. Rats scurried they were from Saddam and Gomorrah. Their teeth were venomous because they ate poison that was absorbed by their system and their bodies brought it out venom. They broke down humans and ate them. The animals from Saddam and Gomorrah had computers that was expensive. The computers had time travel recreation. The animals had availability to live s humans in society did.

Upon sleeping the venomous rodents covered Joker. He was alarmed. He scurried them off killing one before it bit him. The process was death moving in trying to sleep and rodents coming eating him. Joker was tough and thought looking. He consumed the rodent fur and all. He knew it was the only way to live. The venom placed him between life and death. His fever was high he lay on the bunk and placed blanket over him. He shivered and broke down. He did no pray. His mom taught him that God was suspicious a fairy tale was the Bible to his family only. His mom stated to him there was no proof that God or eternity existed. He was out for two weeks mostly a coma upon waking a rate was next to his bed looking at him. It was venomous. He smashed it with all his might and strength knocking the rodent out. Red blood oozed out as he completed the kill. The bathroom was stocked with toilet paper and the shower held enough water for ten showers. He ate the second rat. He took a shower after drying off. He collapsed. The venom hit hard. Joker slid to his bunk and passed out. He covered up. The ocean boomed and the computer creaked. The prisoners were moved, Joker was delusional. He would never come back from the venom. The animals set up compete created them in Exxon. The dead guard attracted them there were over two million venomous devil roaming Exxon.

Havana had a big population and somehow repeated one thousand. The location went on trillion into the future of years. The spider kingdom was the enemy. The population was trillions. The thought the problem was they liked marvel comics too much. Some products repeated somehow. Havana was 0702, a population that was in existence before our plant weather considered. Before the Garden of Eden, Saddam and Gomorrah or however scholastic recorded time. Somehow marvel comics made t. If movies were made the location agreed to be in the movies. Recall was God himself; no one knows how worlds and planets were drawn out in record or people that signed for the movies. The actors were picked, what the recipient received was immortality on the silver screen. They signed for how they wanted to look. Dirty Harry signed, she was 17, brilliant, and built well. Harry Callahan said, "Hi, I'm Harry. I'm known. Females know me. I was done by a female one only me. You know me." Harry was known well. He was 68. He thought that he was 80, he kept up none. He was vigorous and made love that day. "No rope burns." Lisa Caldwell stated. "I was masculine wasn't I? "Yes, I want to speak with the Joker." I liked Harry enough to die for him. I don't want him with anyone else. She died in five minutes. Women highly liked Harry. The death pool ended. It ready Harry, you're good man don't be kinky or it will end. Harry smiled. He died five minutes later. He thought of old age. He was 68 not 80. In the death pool there were 500 women killed by the Joker. The people turn his badge in. He won the death pool one hundred percent because the administration of women said no kinky or it would have cost him his badge.

He won at everything except he did not know that the women loved him very much because he was Harry Callahan FBI and his protection unites were high for Gotham. His signature stated Dirty Harry masculine for the movies. "Good morning Havana." Steve Jackson the morning news. "One trillion people died from venomous attacks. The doctor confirmed spiders and snakes from the state zoo. The devils in webs and huge venomous snakes fifty miles out into the farmland of Havana. They injected DNA from the captain of the research scientist. It was in their offspring. They were one hundred percent bigger than any animal. Humans were pray. The spiders were huge and looked like devils. Humans were pray. The victim of the farmland called for an ambulance. The ambulance drivers were crack and there were one mile long out into Havana. Upon arriving they were killed. Nothing lived. The reports came back received no one lived through the state department.

Srgt. Bill Yakel was over the city police of Havana. Populations one million black, whites, and Hispanic. It was crime free. It was called the lost city of Havana because at year trillion it ended one hundred percent. It was not recordable. It sank far into the sun trillions of years ago and was never and was never in existence again. The number of people was one trillion one trillion times. It was lost in time. The Lost City of Havana. Havana drove cars. The cars were upgraded new year after year. Music was intense. The workmanship was high, product was named differently. Cars were different. Marvel comics were different; they liked the characters in them because they flew around. Havana loved that they bought two a week and read the colorful comics. They were thirty pages intriguing the citizens of Havana. Though y read millions in lifetime Havana's cash came from the distribution of comic books. They loved marvel because they made money from comic books. The comic books were registered from Gotham a location that ended one trillion one billion the rest of your life, lots of people. The comic books were titled Gotham with the Joker. They thought of the Joker as a clown with a bad attitude. Gotham sun went out when the oxidation ran out.

Bill Yakel asked for help with any criminal resign from other police department and with the death of one trillion. In the fifty mile radius they were very much afraid. In Havana it was twice as big as the United States. The school teacher Lisa Adams taught eighth grade. She was built well and pretty. The mountains were purple hue and cast venom one hundred percent. The woods were farmland and full of a to z. Every predator of the spider and snakes world and examples were an Eagle with fangs of venom. They jumped from trees and made noise at night. They were in fifty miles of country. "Hi Havana, the students of the eighth grade. We have an animal problem. We have to stick together for an output that is good." Lisa Adams smiled. Sebastian Bock was a black widow tarantula that was named Sebastian in the zoos. He gained control of Havana and recreation from God of Havana. He was treacherous and mean. He would kill anything alive. He left kids alone. Jed Clampit was the only army that would kill kids because he went out on tax invasion and thought that they were after his moral fiber.

Havana had a lot of cities and metropolitan areas. Srgt. Yakel was determined to win over a community that had control of the systems of his country and state. He used programmers some. Their use was to program your computers fine-tuned so output was yours. Some engraved computers and tried for output of state. The state department he asked that his programmer come out with a solution for the spider community and venomous snakes that because their last victim. Yakel shook; he couldn't believe that that beast existed. They intimidated him. He usually knew his boundaries and was intimidated by nothing that believed in case. The venomous devils could absorb and enter any environments. Some went into coves that killed humans and ate them. Spray worked but ten came back if not trillions to check on their kin and usually the spray ran out. There were so many. They came back from computer units of Sebastian recreated mean and an output of death.

Srgt. Yakel processed his computer programs sent by his programmer. There were hundreds. His programmer wrote through programs, designed on movie slots that had output in special effects and time travel. He looked the computer list over. There was a space odyssey that recreated someone in the future. The equal to England that at twenty three went out on tax invasion.

Randy Jones

The recreated someone in the future. The equal to England that at twenty three went out on tax invasion. They recreated him one trillion years before he was born, at age forty. Al he did was walking the streets Otto. The space travel units were successful upon the recreation of Ottol they kept him in a dry cell and urinated on him. Boiled spat on him and laced his food with poison. They were cruel to him for an unbelievable amount of time. Otto was high in IQ. All he did was ask if his money was good in the government. At 80 he deceased of hundred and starvation. The queen had buried him under a tree written was poor man died. She thought that he would admit that at twenty three and become an aspect of the state and regain tax invasion was permanent for Otto.

Did you go out on tax invasion? The leader of the space expedition asked. Otto's moth was open in reply. He went out one minute later. He did not know the outcome. "Put him in the stock aid with chicken parts for an eternity of punishment." He waved his hand. "Does that mean off with your head?" "No, it means you may go." Otto went into a dry cell. He was fed chicken. Srgt. Yakel received the program somehow. He reviewed it. Ottesmecta for the first time before his birth.

Jed Clampit was probably around during any space exploration past, present or future. He was a hard case that one year after tax invasion has his mom who suggested he make certain his taxes were paid in Milwaukee later. He moved down to the southern state of Birmingham Alabama. He was tax devoid. One year later he has his mom who he called granny mark of the beast. She died and was recreated Satan. If you believe the mark of the beast occurred before end of time revelations and it did. Jethro a college student received Satan and Elly Mae later became Janey Pruitt. She had ten kids that were alive from Satan and mark of the beast. They turned out evil guns and everything. They were confederate army generals. Jed Clampit liked them very well. Upon receiving the mark of the beat Jed refused it. He said tax invasion was enough after granny received the mark of the beast.

Jed Clampit, the Milwaukee oil man that wore a big floppy hat. He smiled and said, "You did it Mae. I am a tax recipient. My organization is confederate army." The confederacy judges on all issues of God in government on tax invasion on Jed Clampit. I will issue more incentives than anyone. Jed's mom Clementine Clampit was college educated. The song that made it through time a real life version was "Oh my Darling, Oh my Darling, Oh my Darling Clementine." It spoke of Jed after tax invasion. You were gone forever oh my darling Clementine. Jed brought the confederate army recreated from hell. No one ever guessed that he ran the biggest army and most successful of all time. If you really believed that Satan injected, that means he was a fictional or superstitious that you never met in your life time. That was determined head administration over the Middle East and communism and Jed Clampit tax invasion. If you did not accredit them you lost the organizations did whether superstitious because one mythological approach was horns and a tail. Jed was real. He was stated high in Satan's classification. In a life time you never met the dark prince.

Srgt. Yakel cleared his desk. "What do you think about our serpents out in caverns and jungle terrain, of our devastated farmers Kate Flannigan?" Kate Flannigan was his secretary. She was pretty yet plump in the behind. "I wore insulation that caused weight gain because men found my form enticing." He looked at her, "What do you think is a solution to our serpents out in the jungle?" Yakel was euphoric. "I don't know", she said. Srgt.Yakel's office door was locked. The lights were turned off. His computer flashed neon. The environment was 1977. Kentucky Fried Chicken and metropolitan areas of civilization, 1977 Ford LTDS Buick, Mack Trucks, and traffic lights.

Dirty Harry's sales were high under Clint Eastwood; Don Johnson of Miami Vice played Dirty Harry next. The sales were median and a third Rick Marcum was a young Dirty Harry. Don Johnson played Colombo Peter Folk was one original. He played a role of Al Capone in the Untouchables. The computer ran the city of Los Angeles. The Gotham Illinois is flashed the location where one trillion billions of time before. The planet Earth and the United States. The computer had entered. Recreate Dirty Harry Callahan. Everything Dirty Harry appeared his organization sort of like a cartoon animated character. He was boxed for recreation and his son Stetson.

The country was jungle terrain was infested with tarantulas underground in caves. Snakes all sorts of devils and devil spiders. He peeked out of an underground trench. He wore clown makeup and looked like venom; nobody knew anything about the Joker's race. He was an event that went with the zoos a to z. Killer serpents weather bred from wilderness and captured or if the state modified them in under kill reptiles. Joker was a faucet of an entrance that went with the zoos of Saddam and Gomorrah. The ended one trillions of times in the future. Trillions of years ago. It was brought in by the creator and listed the most evil time ever. Joker copied the terrain in the country.

Hi, I'm Stephen Timper our coffee is for sale. He drove to Stephen Timber's gourmet coffee shop. "How's the coffee Mae Mae?" He said smiling. He was twenty seven and straight Italian. He worked coffee through one hundred through a program. "Hi, Mr. Timber you are tame in your output a pussycat." The Italian Don smiled. He was from Italy and behaved like it. "Why don't you open two places and give one to me." She said. His wife smiled. Stephen is a good man from Italy. "He's tame." Rachel replied. "I'd like to beat him with a stick." His wife smiled. "Stephen is a good man, her name was Tammy Timber. Rachel was nineteen, and a very pretty. "You're tame, tame, and tame and I would like to beat you with a stick." She used profanity's unbecoming a Don. Timber was fluent Italian. Don a killer from Al Capone's ancestry that was different in output. He sounded like a cartoon skunk. If he were deadly Peppy La Pu. People districted or filed his Italian ancestry as to America. They thought that he was tame. He put up with nothing in his coffee shops that were highly successful thirty years before Starbucks.

"You are a sissy Mr. Timber." He had a .38 that went out of his sock almost into his hand and he fired. "Oh my God." She said I was wrong and slumped down dead moments before employment. She signed government games against Al and signed her X. She thought that she could take advantage of people. It was a form of Satanism; people thought that for example you could advantage of people. It was go gin to Satanism. They believed the government backed them. They called it signing in the state. They thought that they had state protection you do if you are harmed and call the city of state police. "I want Timer out of commission. I would like to kill him with a gun and his ancestry." Rachel signed stage on she swayed her head to the side stage on stage off.

Send a patrol out to see if Timber is legal or not. Is he from Italy? She stated yes. His wife Tammy is from Italy also. The state police pulled into Timbers drive. He walked up the drive. "Hi, Stephen Timber." The officer stated. "Are you legal in coffee sales?" The state police asked. Timber presented a gun and fired. Timber picked the body up and placed it in the dumpster. He drove to the coffee shop. Rachel was carried out by Mark Lyons mafia hit man for Al Capone. There were eight waitress left. They were setting up the coffee shop. They thought that Rachel would be back. The waitress was ten that signed to take the Sicilian Don Dawn. How the Sicilian won was they killed cops and would not be arrested. "Hi, I'm Brenda. Slut girl over there should be dead." "Are you talking about my wife?" Timber asked. "Yes." She said. "She liked you, is it time to meet Ma Timber?" Twenty three asked. He knew no better because that what you call them in Italy. When their wife Timber was cutting cheese, cheese from Italy. It was expensive. He would try a pinch and give it to everyone else.

"You are a sissy." Brenda stated. "Ma ma you are a bitch, I'm telling John Gotti you're a fake. You're under stage 3. I'm killing everything of yours by pretending." New York work up with Maxwell House. It was good regular was one hundred percent caffeine. Dec was Dec. Timber's coffee had not arrived. It was good regular was one hundred percent caffeine. "Good morning our Louisville Don is my brother Stephen Timber. He's a cat. He's my little brother. I'm the oldest." John Gotti was 23 all of the Dons were the same age. There were a million of them. Each had one million men. "Please buy Timber coffees."

The srgt. Went back to his office. His computer was flashing civilizations of the United Sates. The year in the Lost World of Havana was one trillion. The playback showed the country equal to fifty miles of Colorado, the hills were green; it fed off the streams that ran dry during the summer. Saddam and Gomorrah showed the location that Joker was from. Saddam and Gomorrah year one trillion one trillion time after the Lost City of Havana.

"Good morning, I'm President Casey. We have trillions of blacks off the street that need food please make sure they are fed." President Casey was black. No blacks were starving. "Hi, I'm Rick you have to place alcohol to the side and live life without it." Rick was black. The president modified blacks in the counsel. The president also lied about the black's food intake. There were ten main districts of all races, one million people was in counsel for alcohol. "I'm Senator Williams." The time was 6:15 a.m. The beverage for breakfast or wake up was coffee grown in Atlantis the Los Sea an original with one trillion people that made it through time. Trillions upon trillions of years and could be in existence today. The coffee, hot tea and chocolate came from Atlantis. The coffee was the same as Columbia to the United States. I was President Byers our district was ten. Atlantis was processed one trillion miles under a sea that was ink. It survived the Holocaust, after the Holocaust and went into the future after the Saddam and Gomorrah. Their involvement in was fare was none.

President Byers had a square meal for breakfast. The breakfast orange was mango frown in the citrus aspect of Atlantis. It went on trillions of miles into terrain that was governed by the state of Atlantis. The growth enhanced the citrus supply one hundred percent. It was grown by computer with spoil that was specified. President Byers at the mango. He went to business meetings. His output was high in business. He met with the clergy that served God and wanted mango production high. President Byers had output from Atlantis one hundred percent. His morals were high. He wore regular clothes to the year far into the future. He had three kids. His wife loved him very much. She looked like Kate Jackson, who was in the 70's series. The Rookies and Charlie's Angels. Kate Jackson came one trillion years later. School went on in Atlantis and the government was high in output. The seasoned crowd did drugs and prospered from crowds of sex. Having it at the same time. In the United States during the protest and early 60's the protest was the Vietnam War. The spoke of group sex and called them orgies. Saddam and Gomorrah had ten gymnasiums full of participants. The sign read: Gomorrah Sex is Sex and it read Orgy.

The kid populations went up to participants were clean. The police didn't bother them. They went to school and work on time. The product was named one hundred different. The days were long or short. "Hi Commissioner Adams. We have a black situation on our hands. Let's go to Satanism and be bruited and go back one hundred of the whites signed. In government Satanism over blacks. The black population was high and behaved well. The white thought that the government supported them and they didn't. The whites were checked out one hundred percent by the police. Died was one million.

It took two weeks for Saddam and Gomorrah to sign in government and they did. Atlantis was frozen, there was no sign that it existed. The government of Saddam and Gomorrah signed for and went to Satan's tactics one hundred percent never to return. The zoos were let out and the animals contained were venomous and deadly. Joker was their leader. They are of their bodies one hundred percent and killed lots of people and modified evil. The government of Saddam and Gomorrah believed that the zoos would crawl up trees and die.

President Day

Stetson spoke to people as a detective. He was a pro at assessing their cases. He knew and viewed the Dirty Harry's with about ten people playing his dad Harry Callahan, Clint Eastwood, Don Johnson and about eight other actors were successful at playing in the Dirty Harry movies. Harry Callahan showed criminal upbringing upon his friends being killed instead of protected, moods? Maybe. He knew of Sheriff Bufford Pulser who hated blacks because they would not leave town when asked. There were about ten actors from Carol O'Connor to Tom Arnold because the southern sheriff signed for TV or movies. Sheriff Montgomery Scott was in the Heat of the Night. Stetson was a quick study. He knew the eight hour work day and to report back to his office. He brought movie packages to enhance his entrance and exits and to disguise him. There was crime from the mafia to the Hells Angels that his dad Harry Callahan grew up around and modified traits without doing so.

Egypt was at the top of the list, the most deadly upon being initiated was the confederate army. Past, present, future, whether it was Milwaukee in Saddam and Gomorrah or another location the man lost. He then built a confederacy that would take over and win strategies at the end of time. Stetson was civilized. His brother Steve Thomas taught school and went by curriculum and by the state book of history. Once the lights went out on his New York City School and he froze. Egypt a curriculum that was being taught and took the class through the Egyptian Empire. The head pharaoh was Erving Stature and through Steve's transports system. The students went through Egypt piece by piece. Steve had all zones of warfare stored on his computer. He was Dirty Callahan's second son and had a high output in areas of history. There was a big Egyptian Empire a to z. They were the biggest criminals of our time with one millions pharaohs and a big military. The original race was Cuban. The Egyptian military came out of their pharaohs or rabbis of Satan none. Their English was fluent and like Jed Clampit. Their existence was old and traditional weather from Saddam and Gomorrah or what location. The Cuban had a high IQ as Egyptian devils and knew what was happening.

In world affairs Steve Thomas went through the empire, he bothered them none because he was not the military. He listed them under fiction and the facts came in from history. The truth was they made it through time. Freezer units, mummification would imply death and recreation. They were out of units. Alive the confederate army was recreated in the devil out of freezer units. The srgt. Srgt Yakel looked data up. He was a street cop. The woman deceased were five hundred when Harry Callahan was a street cop that went from paraded in Los Angeles and sleeze bars, even ticketing in uniform with crack record to Gotham Illinois.

"Hi Havana. Has a problem with venomous spiders and snake. We are at off end to go against them we have no resistance against venom in our water or our food. The state police escorted or cleared out three locations because Sebastian cleared those locations out because a captain of the police signed for war fare with our stage three with the government. Hundreds of years ago for Havana you tell him you're kidding and wave sideways. It goes off. He died and it went off. We were subjected to stage of warfare only if Sebastian decided." "Good morning doll, you are my wife?" "Hello commissioner you disgust me in some way find out how."

It was hundreds of years earlier. "If you continue to disgust me I'm going to the state department and turning you in." The housekeeping of the commissioner stated the city was Havana. It was the third largest. It was as big as New York. "You turn me in I'll turn you in." His hair was brown, he was forty. He had sex with twice. She was the same. Spanish in the United States. She was an immigrant. She cleaned house very well. He did not pay her when she had sex to keep her mean. The third time she stated, "Sign for stage three and I will not tell that you did not pay me' Maria stated. He was single; she was very good about looking. He knew about stage you sign and a wave sideways took it off. He went to state police and signed his signature, stage three on and off. Maria needed sex, sex, sex. "Are you married?" Captain Robert Corrso asked. "No" the commissioner asked. "Get her name off she's innocent. He circled Maria. His IQ was high and he knew that his commissioner was at stake. He waved that will do, am I commissioner or not?" "You stage the state police will be after you." She was very pretty. He paid her one hundred percent. His life went to zero. She left. He never returned to office and never got anything out political.

"Good morning America, a commissioner signed for stage three. We test him. He doesn't test us." They laughed at political circles. He was a joke because Maria ruined him. He didn't pay her, they laughed. It means the government tests you. She must have been pretty. They showed a picture of Maria, she said that they could. She was wearing her maid's uniform and held the commissioner's head. They needed his permission none because she ruined him and surrendered his life to her. They would ask her. They laughed all political in his. The commissioner laughed. He was ruined and he liked. Till he was eighty he ate cuisine and watched TV. He cleaned his own house. He stated at home. He was happy that he did not have to please people. His IQ was high. He went from one hundred percent as police commissioner to zero. He was happy because Maria, the housekeeping department was paid. His only visitor was a cat, he killed it. He wanted no visitors. Food came by mail. It said do not come out your ruined. Sebastian held that against Havana zero because the commissioner was the only signature. If one hundred percent of Havana had signed the president would have taken them underground and poisoned them. Sebastian was after them because of food supply.

We're the police department, we have one hundred police. "Hi, the police know what they're talking about they are our police of the future.' Barbara Stetson was the fifth secretary of Harry Callahan. Gotham has a lot of excess time on their hands for five hundred women that were rejected by Harry because I don't know how to marry. To ruin Harry was born of AAA baby dolls with too much language and excess time. They were brilliant in looks. AAA triple V was straight. Some of the nude magazines modified behavior of amazon women etc. The point was when sex was through the man's stature or physical output was one hundred percent. The women was sixty percent, hence forth handcuffs etc. Women as well as men were hygiene, restroom etc. Work relationship, sex was shown in public zero. It was considered a Los Angeles game that had AAA supermodels and was a ruin if modified. In the pages of porno, fantasies, sex, etc the cure was straight sex It was unusual business, babes or women in LA would come out Hawaiian tropic chested tight in t shirts that was unbelievable. White bikini bottoms cut off. The walked the beach. Went back after a walk used their restroom in their apartment that as indeed a ruin for a goddess. They watched TV while hopefully the men thought of their well clad boy. Not every male or female though the same, yet they had packages of behavior for Los Angeles sex. If their parents were present it was embarrassing especially for the dad, for his daughters to be scantily dressed. A brother affiliated less with a chest rounded sister build AAA. If sex were known and a goddess placed together well was known public to be the hostess of bondage. The dad mostly died. Introduction to XXX were successful as operas. You saw sex in sell pretty supermodels. Males sold also. Tome Sellick etc. Women got married, men got married. Usually male sports entrusted laughed at friends that stated they licked to be broken down. .Their friend that was broken down got to own up to his defeat by an angel of the beast. When arrogance showed his friend would look at him are you kidding? His take down artist would be pressed in AAA attire. She would be exquisite in form of sensual.

"I didn't realize that you were a prize that you have sex in bed." His friend would quiver. "Go to the bathroom when you come back be yourself." His friend the sports enthusiast would be straight a laugh. "When you have welts on your behind usually you speak of it none. I wasn't unaccustomed to sex. I have two kids. You get out of it at bad realize they are other outlets." He was straight and changed none in a life time. She held her soft hand out. She was tanned and smiled sensually. Her body was unbelievable AAA. She took his hand and stated come one lets go to the bathroom. They guys had great looking women. His eyes got big. Usually they keep sex in the bathroom, not in unfamiliar with LA sex. I'm not like that, any charges by the woman. His girlfriend smiled none, "You're a man." She smiled. She was built well. The baby doll let him to the restroom with her soft hand taking his. I'm going to have to leave him at home. He agreed in bed over my kneed with a paddle to own up to defeat. One of the sports enthusiast looked around. I have kids and do not talk about sex. I never will. I'm not stupid. I wasn't new card player at our card game. The men agreed. Women may have or not ruin attracted to dominant actors, bosses, etc. In a dominant fashion sex was sex and was supposed to be fun. Masculine and feminine, yet it was a sunken sublime in life and went unexplained in certain details that a dominant male would have a friend that their wife would frown upon being anything but male and it would be modified. Sex that was known and announced.

Havana had a snake problem. We can't do anything about it. He went on two hours about the local problem. He was accurate one hundred percent except he forgot women needed restrooms and the location went to bowel. He smiled any questions. Barbara Stetson pointed to a uniformed Harry Callahan, "Harry had a good mind for such situations. Maybe if the state goes my way and the police approve." Officer Mike Richardson smiled. "Anyone incorporated or hired by Srgt. Yakel is a friend of mind." Harry smiled. "Good." The woman we built AAA and pointed restroom. The state police stated go. "Well Barbara isn't you going?" Harry stated. "You killed me Harry by not marrying me." "I didn't mean anything. The srgt. Do you think he's legitimate?" Harry asked. "Yes." Barbara stated. The woman lined up for the restroom. Barbara frowned. "It's ashamed that women don't know when to go to the bathroom Barbara." Harry stated.

Harry was into kinky none. He was straight usually female dominant meant zero because in the movies as well as life they didn't want to see men killed. Yakel the city police officer had gray hair. He was a good shot, his record was spotless. He was smart. The city police was one thousand. His computer was expensive at detail of experts in the field. The computer brought back Harry. His captain and thousands of FBI agents from Gotham Illinois. Five hundred of his women that were the death pool of secretary, his two sons were in with their wives. Stetson was in a nice house not far from the police station. He smiled at his wife that was gunned down by the Cubans. I never thought that I would see you again. It's great. He was happy even euphoric. She was happy. "I love you; I'm allowed to be here in Havana with you and your dad harry. Maybe we can help." His wife stated. He looked at her, he loved her. "Maybe we can help, I hope so."

Steve Thomas, Harry Callahan's other son lived closed to the university not very far from Srgt. Yakel. His wife placed together a lunch, "Do you think that we can help?" Steve ate. "I hope so, I work at the university and my assignments is to bring the university in Stetson. To bring information in dad to absorb and arrest the FBI to absorb the enemy and prosecute. The secretaries were five hundred. Secretary's built AAA that worked for the state department. Dirty Harry's girlfriend that had his two kids was in the house with him. Sebastian. Then he was reentered by the srgt. He had no memory. Yet his strategies were really good.

The miss from Havana was the confederacy that causes the War Between the States. Jed Clampit's confederate army came one trillion one thousand times. In the future chances were the confederate army was handled well by the city or state police and it got out of hand. They were good at handling situations such as tax invasion. Havana went on trillions o years past. The country was a terrain where giant spiders were the same as wolves in a wilderness. The population was none. The buildings were abandoned. The grasses grew high and the weeds.

"Hi, I'm the police department those ten uniformed police are friends of mine." "The venomous spiders and snakes are out of circulation for now. They went back into their caves for now. I would like to welcome Dirty harry amongst the police force." Dirty Harry tipped his hat "Hi." Dirty Harry was in a police uniform. The uniformed officer that was the speaker continued, "We are at a standstill. We need help from all police." "It's coming," said Dirty Harry. "I have two million FBI on standby upon the captain's orders." Havana's schools went on political was slowed yet went on commerce was up. Marvel Comic sells were high, cinemas were extra high because Batman was shown before and after in a cape. They loved marvel comics. The movies and stock were different. Steve Thomas brought the school the school systems in; he was capable through the police department. He resided in a security office. Stetson secured the military with the permission from the president. He resided in a security office. Stetson secured the military with permission from the president. The state police and the city police there were thousands that died a day. They went into their hose and killed them and became them. The devil stayed inside forever. They ate real meat only.

The srgt. Got official power from the government for Harry to take charge of the assignment against the killers. The secretaries of the death pool sent memos of information to Havana on behavior where to go. How to behave to avoid being killed. The devil killers were two million spiders, two million snakes. There were lots. They were sprayed and returned twenty four hours later recreated. Harry began work on a screen that went around ten cities and memos went out by the secretary's to move into one of the ten cities. Steve Thomas brought in the school system. Stetson the military through the state police with the equal to the National Guard. Helpful only helpful there were trillions. It took two weeks to place a screen around the city. Infrared brought venom in of people killed and become by the devils. They were shot and taken out by the officers. There were millions. One million officers were killed. The screens were installed and the order was to spray with high powered insecticide. Dirty Harry wrote into a notebook, like a doctor that prescribed medicine to a disease. Harry had a good mind. The mother to his sons met with their sons for food, Harry liked her.

The team of Harry Callahan with millions of FBI countered the spider problem. The srgt shook Dirty Harry's hand. "You are an aggressive office of the law." He shook Harry's hand, "Your sons are a crack image of their dad." Harry smiled. "Glad we could help." Harry walked out of the srgt's office. The devils of the country are out of the way. He cracked his knuckles and placed powder on his hand like a weight lifter that kept the bar from slipping. After pulling his sleeves up, the powder took sweat off his hands. He typed into the computer return Dirty Harry. The team was returned. Steve Thomas and his wife were returned to New York. They had non memory. Stetson was back in the office. The srgt tried to erase memory. Stetson was frozen and in freezer units and out with a report of Havana. He had memory. He returned to his detective office. What bothered him was he was used, without pay by the srgt of Havana, a lost world in time.

Timmy mulled around Stetson's office. She was married one year earlier. Stetson went to her wedding. He looked over his docket for scheduled cases. "What bothered you the most about Havana and seeing your dad?" She asked. "What bothered me was we did a crack job without pay. Brother and I called him. He has no memory. Steve and I didn't remind him." He frowned. "I wonder if Havana made it through time Srgt Yakel." He was manipulative usually the police are honest it's a code isn't it? "Usually." Stetson stated.

There were twenty four contracts on oil leases in San Antonio Texas. The year was 1928. "We have to hit high." Eric Erving stated, "But how can we validate our money?" He wore a Stetson hat that looked like a straw hat. He was twenty three. His build was good. He contributed one hundred percent to his family. They appreciated it none. The government paid and they needed no money. He paid electric and water and set smoke alarms. His age was twenty. The family was ten. His mom and dad included there were twelve. He was trained in oil and worked oil. His education was Yale, he was taught to show education none. If asked if education say yes I'm educated. His IQ was high.

Al Capone was in Manhattan, a man said he wanted him dead. He went in and said "Why do you want Al Capone dead?" "I don't" Jake stated Al drove back to Chicago. He was happy. Al was twenty three. His interest was crime syndicate, Sicilian Mafia Chicago. His money was good and he wanted to keep it that way. His money was thirty million. That was like trillions all day in present time. His money was legal in the United States. In the bank and by the state department. He did not go out on tax invasion because he signed nothing. The reason he was known to be the biggest criminal of all time was because he won over tax invasion. His IQ was high, extra high. He won every case of crime. He knew how to behave before and after. His mafia was on trillion, his occupation since twelve was black market sells in guns it was legal business until 1977. On being shot he wondered why you would shoot him. He sold you a gun. Al was real quick with guns. He won one hundred percent with guns. He knew no better. He was involved in to her matters outside of Al Capone none. The reason he won was he was quick with crime. His victims showed up in the papers one hundred percent dead. They deputized themselves, said the state department backed them and decided to kill Al because he went out on tax invasion. There were at least two million they were illegal. There were judges, politicians, attorneys, and school teachers. He relaxed after they were dead. Al's name was centralized Chicago and they thought that he liked to play games.

You hit oil Eric Erving the police officer informed him. Big you have a millions dollars coming. He smiled. That's grate a million dollars was like a trillion present day. "Where do I pick it up?" Eric asked the police officer. He wore the straw Stetson hat. It had a patch of blue denim. The police officer found it revolting. He asked why a hat. "Sorry officer. I was in the oil business; do you want me to take it off?" "No wear it. I will buy crude is unrefined. Please buy refined." Eric smiled and shook his hand. He was 6'3" and gangly on when oil went down. He recovered in a week your money's good in America. The uniformed police of Dallas Texas got into his car and rode off. He bought refined oil from Eric only.

Erving Stature got out of bed. His stature was big. He ate breakfast. The food was edible from America, England tried him rarely. Their money was distributed from America's U.S. gold made it good through franks. The gold and jewelry was expensive for the prince to show only. He went into the foyer. His palace was expensive. His money was trillions. Good in America. He was served breakfast by the staff. He spends ninety eight percent of his life in freezer units and came out on a B. His staff was good at conducting business. His shaven head was groomed with olive oil by servants. He had a sexual for one, she was built A. He dressed in robes of Satan and chanted curses to the military. The pharaohs were one million and they followed orders one hundred percent. In freezer units they were Cuban devils. The spoke American as a first language. They wore dresses as original Egyptians on present level. They knew no better than to be Egyptians with shaven heads and stature of six feet tall. They did everything. They were very good with their fist. Their military was frozen with them and gained on American warfare upon commercializing Egypt one hundred percent. Their kids were a lot and were raised Egyptian they were frozen at eighteen and came out a foreign character of Egyptians. They stayed young. Egypt's number was trillions. They retained little of number one criminal because they killed in Egypt name. In Satan's name, the United States thought they were tame.

Dallas Texas

Eric was married to Barbara Smothers. He bought a ranch that was worth two million because it was sturdy. He ran cows and goats and made a bundle off goats, goats were just in that year. He was real expensive at everything and won one hundred percent of the time because he was sturdy in deals. He drove a Rolls Royce worth millions and ate caviar for breakfast. His IQ was high. Barbara didn't think right or she would have fixed him a big breakfast she never learned to cook. Her age was twenty three. Dallas Texas met an oil man that would never lose. He ever knew how. He was big everywhere. His name was Jock Erving.

JR Ewing woke up. "Good morning daddy. How much money do we have?" JR asked Sue Ellen was scantily dressed, she was built A1. He knew that none because he knew her his whole like and knew no better. His money was thirty million and he was excellent at business. "Don't worry about money JR, it won't run out." Jock wore work boots and a Stetson hat. "I signed for the movies and the name will be Dallas." Jock shook his head, "Make sure." "I'm Dallas, a fine and outstanding citizen in Burbank. I did not sign for stage 3. The government tries you on organized crime if they try you without a signature their saying you are light. Kill the leaded of the political and become him and you win. If not they try you for one hundred years. They say your leader is a sissy if the president gets by with it they will try you for one hundred years. If you win you are gifted by God." Freeze your organization and bring them back. They will tell you if there is anything on in government if there is

Randy Jones

wave your career goodbye. Political come in a text you by stating they are your boss. Just wave your criminal life away. The only one who won was Adolf Hitler won barley. "That's right daddy, all you have to do is wave sideways and hug in and give everything upon and kiss but of political and pray the military doesn't kill you with a gun when you go against the president. I like people that support the president not oppose, or I'll come in with a gun and kill you." Haddam Hassan won that they took him to court and executed him. JR frowned where in the movies you will look like an oil well man with great prestige me like JR Erving. He smiled.

Alcoholism is a disease that goes into your mind and produces results by making you think that your grandeur. Now JR Erving has estates in Dallas that are billion dollar estates. He assesses oil in detail by the trillions. He smiled. Money belts he has one for every day of the week, one color one another. He's high. In IQ and his output is high. He's smart on intake and output. We need more like him. Rick Maddison had been a counselor in the Dallas clinic for two years. He was crack with psychology. "Hi, treatments good if you treat well you have to put the plug in the jug and decipher information Thomas Well you go to AA. Get a sponsor that's someone that has more recovery time tan you and knows how to speak well to you about recovery. Issues and getting back and forth to meeting. You read the big book that was book written by Doctor Bob and Bill Wilson an alcoholic anonymous. You go to an AA meeting anytime you want to take a drink. You reach conclusions that are beneficial in your life and recover daily by medication and prayer. You devote your free time to recovery issues and you get better. Do not issue people in your lives that are trouble or who drink. Stephanie was a counselor for three weeks. She was pretty. Her hair was red. She dyed it because a boyfriend left her. Why? The reason she became a counselor was because she wanted to help people in troubled times. The treatment center had twelve people who were alcoholic. They though well and processed well after three weeks." "Hi I'm Ted Russell Erving. I was Jock's brother. He was in treatment for three days. I want treatment. He drank cognac three times a day, an equal to one pint. He was an alcoholic since twelve." It took one hour and a half he was given plasma and tranquilizers for his stomach that was upset. He went through it's for two days and was sober in three.

At his first meeting he confessed that he was Jock Erving and laughed. His hair was brown and curly. He was a big man. Forty pounds overweight.

84

Jock had been dead for two weeks; he was seventy eight when he died. He said, "JR you're willed out. Treat your Mae well." The chairman said, "Hold it, you are Russel. Say you are Russel." He smiled. "I am Russel, I drank my rights to the Erving Empire up." Russel stated. People laughed, "You are a heavy set Erving with curly kinky hair. Come on JR will sweep the street with you. He's so rich." Russel smiled. "I am Jock's brother. I ate all the Erving's profits for one day and that's a lot of profits. The meeting wends down and out because they liked JR and not Russel because he was immunized poor and JR's rich. He went to treatment and went to meetings and stayed sober somehow. JR asked that he didn't speak about him at meetings because he promoted himself. Russel was sixty four.

Meetings are good if you stay sober. The counselor Tina Marcum was seventeen, she spoke of recovery issues well after care meant you went back after you completed treatment and check in with the doctor and counselor on your progress. She spoke for five minute on how to stay sober. She quit when Russel asked who was the most successful. Himself or Russel, himself her mouth opened and she said, "You are serious Russel, JR could swat you and kill your whole family." Russel's education was college. The state played for Jock's family and they were happy. They didn't understand why Jock would try to promote money for them. Russel was educated under the clean hygiene. In Dallas ruling he went in his clothes were cut in half and received college. He went in thirty six hours and learned a lot about college education. He liked to read up on it and keep up in class. Hygiene was an aspect of life. He found out he graded an A and liked it. He improved his reading skills and Russel Erving got an A. The teacher said, "Keep your clothes were his clothes. They tried to give him a new pair of pants and Russel tore them up. "Hi sober is good Russel are you done with JR?" He smiled. "Yes he can take a break since Jock died. I run his estates." He smiled. "I guess he can do whatever he wants." She smiled and said, "He's very successful." Russel Stover fat boy, she pointed she was built AAA.

"No Russel Stover, I am not a candy. I'm not fat you are." Russel smiled. The counselor left. You are not JR quit comparing yourself. JR went to treatment twice. "You are supposed to bring jelly beans and speak well of me." Russel told JR. JR looked scolding, "You're my dad's brother aren't you? Why would you talk about you me?" JR asked. "Because in the past you spoke of me and my family like they were trash. You should have given money to your son and treated Sue Ellen well. Bobby and Pamela should have had kids." Russel smiled. "I guess I won't talk about you." JR frowned, "Jelly beans the next time." "None unless you make them from scratch and you don't look like Jock. You look like me." Russel stated and took a drink of his decaf. "I didn't think that you could have coffee. Can you check with the nurse?" JR was spiteful because Jock was mentioned a he didn't say he was a good man. "It's decaf." Russel held his hand out for a hand shake. "No you're trash." JR left. "Spiteful behavior." JR went to AA meetings twice when Russel stated that he would pass JR up.

Years earlier JR was at school. Jock went to pick him up. JR's family tree showed Russel with a joint of marijuana in his mouth and a beer. It said trash. Russel was involved in better hygiene. He looked at it said, "JR I could do you like that don't print me dumb." He shook a finger at him. The next time Russel saw him two years later JR had a Mercedes Benz on the back it said, "Russel Stover is a monk priest that was fed by the state." Russel pointed no. The third time JR had a party with executives and said Russell Stovers is pure price fed by the state. Russel laughed and said, "I won't compete you." JR was called by the chairman in AA stating Russel Erving was competing. Miss Elly an aging woman said, "Russel you are trash." "Miss Elly." Russel tipped his hat. Ray the hired hand said, "Trash." Russel said, "Behave yourself, you are help for the Erving's. I am an Erving." JR looked mad. Watch what you say about his brother Jack. "Okay Erving's leave." The Erving's left. JR went to AA, don't talk about me. All he said was he was Jock and would catch up with JR.

Russel was sick in treatment and going through withdraw. .It took one year of recovery before he got a grip on his life. The reason he spoke of JR was during the family tree he said trash becomes Jock when he died and I'll break you down trash. JR remembered it and was kidding. Russel was kidding. He liked JR immensely well because he was a good business man. He was for Jock one hundred percent of his lifetime. They thought that Russel hated them. Jock's whole family liked JR. He knew that none. How they showed it was they said they liked him.

JR was in his office. "Bill Taker made a lot of money and he tried taking from my daddy funeral precession. We need to flag him and put his money in our bank. He gained off the Erving's." Bill Taker went in and saw JR. He was wearing a tux. He was going to a wedding of friends. "Hi JR." Bill Take spoke. "What do you want sir? You made thirty million from the bank. JR took it and gave it to the state. Bill went back to his house and stayed. He made money in other business. His IQ was high. He was Pamela's brother. She had three. JR knew how to check up on business oil. He was educated high and his dad taught him and trained him well. JR's finances were one trillion. The money was big. Lucy, his niece was two million. Miss Elly had twenty eight million, she went after him only that Bill Taker should be placed to work. He was a good man and a good business man JR said he was a baby and could quite being a baby. Bill was a good business man.

The spider was a black widow with big fangs, she was good at being wild as a female to males that promoted big in National Geographic showed greenery with drops of rain and a to z venomous spiders that ate birds. She crawled down the web ate the male and went recluse. The egg satchel came out two weeks later, all spiders were eaten except for a black widow tarantula and a dragon. The dragon was a black widow male that dominated time by eating all the other spiders. He bites his mom disguised. He boiled her out and ran across a wed that belonged to his family ancestry was a big black man. He ate him for one year killing off everything that went against him. Killed were one trillion back widow tarantulas, three humans and a government that went to Satan to kill him. His name on his ID was Joker Callahan. Callahan was a special breed of spiders that killed females and everything that went against him the government said stage on he said I didn't sign and waved society ended in three and a half minutes. He was three how he lived was he went to freezer unites and had a medical computer. He ate the bodies one by one. It took over one hundred years He hung in a web and ate of human. He was high in IQ. The location was called Tim Brook. He recreated the next planet. He got recreation from God. He came and said who needs food, the Joker took everything from him and he said you can have this universe. He put his glasses on straight. I want your kit and caboodle. Joker said. He smiled. "You have this universe at the end you won't exist on a recreation because your breed is spiders. You have no soul just a lover of humans as a meal. I will recreate when you're done and drop you out dead." "We'll see Jehovah." Jehovah was seen at this location none, guilty of being a spider. Time went on, went on one with a hundred zeros. It was hard to believe how long it went on because Joker was prudent as survival skills. Joker conquered for one hundred zero one quarto years. He did from lack of oxidation. There was nothing left alive in that universe, another universe was created one trillion years. The rest of your life.

Randy Jones

JR Erving was fifty upon him and his family sneaking in underground. The Federal Bureau of Investigation froze him and his whole family. It was a form of death upon him and his whole family. It was a form of death upon being frozen. It was a death, JR's money sat in the bank one trillion dollars. The year 977. JR said, "I just don't want to die." The FBI knocked his western hat off. It was expensive. "You messed up. You're big though, I'll see you in the movies." The last thing he said was, "Jesus was good. God was good. But why did daddy die?" Was the last thing JR said. One hundred percent of his family was frozen. Jock was frozen at sixty eight. The series Dallas with Larry Hagman playing JR Erving was a success and also with Don Johnson playing the next JR and a third that looked like the original. There were ten. The most successful was Don Johnson. The success of JR Erving, Jock Erving, and Eric was high.

Indiana Jones was a team that was placed together to research and pick up worlds from the archives and dig was like our gold in giving currency validity in America. Recall of the archives was societies that ended to dig up ruins one of the favorites was prehistoric time. The meat eaters and the vegetarians in dinosaurs. The greenery, the caves, fossilization such as leaves imprinted and the dinosaurs sinking into the tar and sun. Research dug up for the most part Egypt. The mummification, drafts of chirographic. Egyptians were shown with jewelry, hats that were emeralds and gold. They showed Egyptians embodied in gold with gems and the equal to empire attire that was cut off for the male. Mummification was important. The jewelry and wrappings of the dead. Egyptians were none embalmed. In mummification they were frozen through time. It was a myth that the Egyptians were placed in tombs. The research team for the team named after a theme park of National Geographic. Discovery of exotic locations ride at Indiana Jones went into caves and wondrous location around the world.

The team of Indiana Jones was school professors trained in their hobbies or field the lead or supervisor was Tim Matthews. He asked permission from the state department of the theme park. Indiana Jones to use the name Indiana Jones as a teacher. They let him. The team assembled in a meeting room at the school. Rick Adams looked at the assembly. They were dressed well. He smiled, "Welcome." "I'm Rick Adams." "Indy." The men chanted. Rick held his hand out in silence. They liked him. They were friends and buddies and like him a lot. "We are a garage band that will have to practice." The school

88

teacher, all professors, all men applauded. The archives, the digs were a hobby. If the outlet made money it would be nice.

Tim Matthews signed for movies to be made under a name he and his organization went by, Indiana Jones. Steve was incorporated on the team. The teachers from different locations of the United States was a team mostly, an organization for fun and if their digs made money. Steve's warfare in a computer and watched war zones when he got off work. He spent time with his second wife Barbara. He fed the fish in an aquarium that had expensive fish and décor of caves. He set the fed to be released for three weeks and had a bac that automatic supply that lasted longer. The lights were set automatic in the mornings. It was cleaned and kept clean regularly. There was a bar set automatic in the mornings. It was cleaned and kept clean regularly. There was a bar set with expensive liquor. Steve drank seldom. He liked exotic drinks that brought an environments of exotic islands. He would have loved his brother Stetsons occasion when he opened a detective agency with spiced paradise of tropical food, drinks and a band set. Those locations existed was somehow imposed in commercialization's as smart or stupid or very expensive. He kept the aquarium well. His wife knew how to buy the right type of foods. Occasions however buffeted food with the right rice's and meats and breads that fit all occasions. They liked bead, you would say, yet beads were dispensed at tourist attraction. The hippy era of the sixties and seventies was shut down not on protest but because drug use protest of the war seemed futile yet there were a lot of cause and effect from the Vietnam War to the Richard Nixon presidency. Shown were American citizens being tear gassed by the police, in protest of the war. Wars would seem to make more sense if the public knew why we as a country knew the absolute reason of the war. Had a design as a country that produced safety for the innocent United States citizens incorporated guns, planes and uniforms to a military trained in warfare against a country that we didn't offend with language barriers or prejudice terms. Religion none unless ask a country bought that classification and incorporated it in their own state department of foreign. In the United States religion was legal through our United States state department because it was safe to consume suggested high morals and you were legal in that area by the state police. If the Middle East ask for religion in their area bought and paid for in their state department their country would then incorporate it. There would be less charges if rejected, no sell no go. If for example ministers were sent there, there may be a language barrier or the country may through flight be prepared for tourist only. The state department man of a Middle Eastern country should provide food, clean clothes and hotel accommodations.

The United States state department handled areas professionally. If charges were checked with leaders that were educated in the United States state department and the Middle East we had a military and had a good record through history. The Middle East was fierce at warfare also, if a language barrier happened to go after trade was paid go and do not go back unless they bought more product more known was free food. To the hungry was dispensed by the state department, not churches, it showed somehow that the state paid for food, food harvest, hospitalizations somehow and churches if the ministries was involved in foreign on trade. They may insult country's that could pay. If we sought pay and didn't involve religion, if in warfare we were safe from an over take. If we fully understood why we were at war and were prepared with a military that reported in detail to the state on actions that kept foreign from overtaking a country innocent of charges. If the military could validate every death that the foreign military would kill what American or takeover what in America our warfare would be validated because American citizens of want protection from a military paid for by tax money from a register that taxes goods in a super market or field taxes on tax day. We want protection from an overtake by military trained in our country to defend from foreign takeover and skills to prevent from a country that trades foreign.

Steve's aquarium changed scenery from caves to wondrous Hawaii. It was breathtaking. The background cooled or warmed, it had a specialized fan that made it seem like the oceans wind came in. Steve spent some time in this location. He had an office or a den to grade papers. His wife, Barbara, stated when you die, I want that aquarium. Steve looked at her. He resembled his dad in features, "Take it now, avoid the rush, and remember that your legal time is Halloween for grave robbery." Steve looked at her as if he was serious. Barbara was enchanting if enchanting was neutral state of feminine that made her happy. Her husband was home. She chose her words differently. She wanted herself and Steve to use the aquarium. She smiled. "I don't want to be dug up, got dug up sometime in the future?" Barbara asked. Steve smiled. "I don't want to be dug up, what's this about, did you watch Dallas or Columbo?" Dallas is on number ten, that played JR Erving and I believe Columbo is looking for someone else. Don Johnson played fully. Dallas comes in with women playing Jane Ewing and all races of masculine and famine. It gives variety. The female version acts, the male black behaves well as a black JR Erving. His panic race played him well. Steve tried to keep his career up. The state he was considered as a school teacher. He kept money in for bills. He was very academic in a professor type of way. People kept up with computer graphics, computer programs some. Central America seemed to like TV much, movies where popcorn probability sometimes thick red carpeting or then listing of titles of movies as you open the doors and enter for the movie paid. The sound was high. It equalized to the movie people usually like drama, they stated we don't talk about movies, series and books. Yet they did. Sometimes they had a book club meeting that varied usually in the movie a to z. They liked events that sold movies and liked to be commercialized themselves.

Steve bought movies in package as did his brother Stetson. To have output in areas of drama, programmers cost, he afford one for a couple hours and pay they were expensive. Steve smiled at Barbara. That female Erving of Ervin oil made you a manipulator. "Those movies come right into your mind on satellite scan. The only thing about it. The Erving's Mrs. Jane Erving did not have their name on a quart of oil." "No." Barbara stated. The Erving's made money though. Barbara winked. It was a to z Dallas. "I was only kidding you because you have a cow lick. You dad Dirty Harry did too." "I hate that that means your hair stands up. The barber or stylist cuts the cow lick out and I moussed it or spritzed it down." Steve smiled. "You can still see it." Steve smiled. "I'm going to go to your work tomorrow and become one of your coworkers. I think they're doing your work because you have too much time to hatch eggs. I'll work that excess off." He pinned her in the nose with his finger. "Tonight with you." She said. She was very desirable. "I was just kidding." "I don't lay eggs, I'm not a frog." Barbara said "No one lays eggs but the serpents of the devil." Steve smiled. "Isn't you?" He said and pointed. "Isn't you?" She said.

"Do you believe that females are DE modified down by babies?" Barbara asked and I was not Jane Erving or pretending to be. I was only kidding. "DE modification is individuals. If you want to DE modify or not." "Oh, it's the college professor, coming out with an opinion on psychology for free." She said. "Thank you, I am a high school history teacher." "Barbara." She said slapping his hand. She was pretty. Her hand was soft. "I'm mostly kidding." Barbara stated. "To demote as an egg layer." Steve smiled. "Or as food for the mom and babies." Barbara was very pretty. "You gain weight or lose the woman is the same in a couple of weeks. You demote or promote accordingly. The changes are you have a kid or a child to look after." "Do you get paid by the states teacher's board or psychiatric mental health. They plug mental health only when they want you to process state and hygiene well. She pointed. "Why a point?" "It's they want you to process state and hygiene well. She pointed. "Why a point?" He implied. "It's close to bed time and you're with a great guy." Barbara smiled. "You forgot my birthday today." She frowned. From under the couch he reached, he had a card and a small present wrapped well. "I didn't forget." He replied. Barbara looked like a cheerleader. She was placed together well, "Didn't forget." He replied. Barbara looked like a cheerleader. She was placed together well, "Didn't forget my birthday." She smiled.

"Hi we are the dairy committee and there are runners that they're not enough cows to supply. The United States that's not true. They're enough dairy cows and enough cows for slaughter to supply the United States and foreign with meat. The runner that saws are soy processed and the carcass goes to the zoo animals of Africa. That is only rumors. The blacks or African Americans are okay with you using Africa. The meat makes it to the zoos is all I'm saying." "Good" Joker stated, "Hopefully the prime cows and livestock will still be sent." He smiled. The chairman stated, "It will go." "Good." Joker was happy. "Why would you care?" He said. The mean maid it and wasn't processed soy. "What do you get fur?" Tim Bates stated.

Joker smiled, "I just want things to go where they go." "I want you out. The ambassador of Africa, a black man. He used a prejudice term." Ted Alan was a black man from Utah, he was surprised that Bates mentioned him. He spoke to him before meeting. He was nice. Please leave the representative of Africa. Does the representative want his name mentioned. "Yes, Ted Alan is my name, please don't make me violent." Tim Bates was a good looking executive. He groomed well, presented himself well in all occasions except he didn't want a black thanks for the report from. He used prejudice names to Ted Alan again." Ted looked at him. Don't talk about me sir or I'll beat you up. Ted said. We met and you were real nice, then what changed. Ted asked. He used a prejudice term and said that you were then and now. If I had a gun Ted said.

"Check that man out." Bates said. Security checked him out. "Do you want him in or out?" "Out." Bates said, "Because he's violent." Ted Alan left. Bates would be robbed every day for weeks because he was very discourteous to a black. The chairman of dairies spoke, "I don't think that we need a representative to

African zoos. The meat makes it, milk makes it." "Jokes wills the zoos still be supplied cows?" "Check him out, he looks criminal." Bates said. "The room was full, the dairy meeting under way." "You'd lose if you have me checked out." Joker smiled. "Because my titles are in order." "Let's see them," the uniformed security stated. "Why did the black guy go?" Joker asked. "Why?" Bates asked.

Joker picked up his ID and passes for the dairy board and put it in his pocket. He seemed supportive of the cows making it to the zoos. Bates looked at him because he was black. "Okay will the cows still make it to Africa ?" "Yes." The chairman said. "Okay, the cows will make it?" The Joker asked. "Confirmed." "We will expect it." "I'm Stetson, was everyone paid? I'm supposed to find out hopefully I'm not out of order." Joker, the Joker began. "I knew your dad, don't get involved. He was Dirty Harry Callahan." The room silenced. They respected Dirty Harry. "I wonder" She was spiteful in relying. "What Al Capone would say she was Marline. Don't get organized crime involved." "What gave me away?" His name was Stephen, his hair involvement. He placed his hand in his pocket, "I stole the," he spaced his words and shot a response, "the integrity of the boss by enjoying his wife. I'm criminal a criminal of love." Go on out the door. Stephen pulled an orange burst lollipop out and took the fine wrappings of clear plastic off and put it in his mouth.

"Go, were you with Stephen?" Rick Albertson asked. "No." She said. "I wonder what Al Capone would have said abut Dirty Harry. I liked him." "Snide." The Joker said, "That you like a cop that would arrest you. You said that you never met an Italian you did not like, he was Italia, and I will spite you by not liking you because you're Italian." Joker was spiteful. "Get him out." Bates said. Joker was having a sour apple lollipop. "Let him stay I want to hear what he says." "Get him out." Bates said. "He went on tax invasion." "No I didn't." Al said. "The people said ninety nine percent. Did you." Joker said "How much money did your end after, get him out." Al Capone gained on tax invasion by killing the state department of Chicago and legalizing himself by a tax department we hired. His money was good, ask Casey. Yes his moneys good, are there any cops that complain? Yes it's good Mr. Capone. Leave Al the chairman of the dairy association because you're a con. Al left because he wasn't welcome. They were note rude in other areas. The mafia wanted him treated rude none.

"Stetson I was hired to find out if everyone was paid." "This, this is Joker, stay out of situations." "Hi, I'm Jones, I was tagged Indiana Jones somehow I was modified through time. Indiana was a different location." He pointed, "Joker didn't sign for movies. Joker didn't in Gotham that came and went. Kolchak did, he was old when he died and didn't want to be recreated." Indy looked like Harrison Ford the actor. We were modified through time straight through Saddam and Gomorrah the reticular and zoo life with fangs and venom took over because the state signed and changed to the devil. Their systems of protection went because instead of modifying crime out they modified it in their training was state. The had no prior training or no way to modify crime against them. The zoos fed off them and their resistance was high than we as humans or them the devil wasn't tangible and crime really broke in and took over. Mankind was weak against a killer society that meat made them pray. IT would be the same for the United States if they went to rime one hundred percent and had no protection on persecution when moral and criminal really moved in. The real McCoy with experience with how to survive with guns or devils from exotic locations with pythons and anacondas that thought like humans centralized and our resistance being human output and their animals, Stetson, Indy continued your brother. Steve from New York is on a team of research. He believes it is named after a theme park in Indiana, however I am an original from Gotham please tell him that the state paid the dairy association.

That's right the chairman told Stetson. Have your boss see me not you. This meetings is assurance we are paid we need to consider a new representative to Africa. Think about it. Adjourned. The dairy association was over. Stetson looked at the record of the state dairy. The money was in the government one hundred percent. They were honest one hundred percent. They stole seldom. Cows were none. The milk sent in from farms none. The contents in the cartons marked milk Stetson looked up soy, soy was grown for miles by farmers. Stetson made a copy of the reports. He dissipated into a B level where the copies were made. He left the report from the dairy affiliation on a B level copied to be sent to his boss. He came out of freezer units back to his office at his house. His programmer watched the process and said well. She was looking into her computer screen. It showed Stetson in his house, He waved. She smiled and the report was into Stetson's boss. She turned the screen off with Stetson home safely. The programmer went to bed, she designed Stetson beyond and peripheral expense in computer program and engineer.

The dairy cows were supposed to be documented in mock, the mock may have been picked up by Joker and eaten by venomous tribes that were known to eat rodents their food supply changed to bigger animals. It was unbelievable how evil the servant devils were. They were political. Joker was the biggest devil he showed up. Trillions of years ago his star burnt out. He was recreated through Indiana Jones and other movies that made it through Gotham. He was capable of taking over the planet before he was hatched out in a Gotham society. His mother was a black window tarantula. His dad a black widow tarantula was killed one trillion years in the future. When he tried to kill Joker. These guys were devil spiders that hung in a web spider were known to die in a short time. These killers lived a trillion years. Joker was fluent at kill. He listed AAA. The worst killer of all time. The killers were a to z in the Garden of Eden, Saddam and Gomorrah, and millions of worlds listing one trillion species.

Joker was the quickest and most lethal of all species. Upon death he came back recreated and watched from the shadows. He went after them only if his name was mention and processed their lives only if they wanted him dead. Gotham year one trillion one billion on checks listed in the year of Gotham. One tried based on the rest of your life trillions. The world of Gotham was future. Counselor Adam Fly had a full congregation. He was high in IQ. "Gotham was big, bigger than the United States. You were to appear in a new world with balloons. Big balloons that you ride in the basket, colorful with the sun gleaming down golden with a perfect hue of blue clouds. You would think for a moment that you were in a perfect location for a parade for you. You stay with nice people that feed you what you like. Maybe banquet in seasoned beef stew first however a salad. So your full and iced cold kool aide. The head of the house hold was male and he along with his tells you about your new location. You are welcome here the parades the costume they were dressed in stage costumes. Rehearsed lined and a crowd to hear them. A mic for auditorium sound. The costumes were fascinating. They had color. The drama couch was the state of Gotham He was a licensed theatrical department hired for plays the states scheduled them and it showed. The light show was expensive. The costume, the actors knew their lines. The crowds were big. The entertainment was high, the event was expensive. The lights were wondrous. The carnival clown judged the spice drinks warm. The holidays cast in orange Halloween neon with environment blue, red brilliant shades. This location went deep into a void. The next was a stare and galaxy. Gotham traces were forgotten mostly.

We of Gotham have a lot of time if we don't promote well. The Joker is a zoo animal, a black widow correct would be black emperor. His kingdom was

Gotham. He was evil. In the zoo it said Joker criminal one. He was a big black spider in a web that was intimidating. He was fifty four in height and as big as a human We saw Joker everywhere. If you stayed with nice people in this location of color and rides that took you through tunnels of time. Air collect to ride through caves and movies instead of universal and paramount was called Sidd Marcum. Presents were presented a to z everywhere there were trillions of them R rated mostly. There was one out of trillions with Joker in it. It showed Joker eating people. The movie went on for two and half hours and sold high at the end. Joker boiled all over the cast and laughed. He went up a web, the loss was he boiled all over the cast. He was paid nothing and asks none if he wanted to be in the movies. He got even by saying he supported it and asking the cast if they supported it. They did and won.

The balloons and carnival environment usually meant well. It was fun, sold was red kool aide a black licorice sold well and speckled eggs. The licorice sold well because it was an appetite suppressant. The kool aide was refreshing. The churches were weird. Satan didn't get created for trillions of years. They had recovery programs for alcoholics, bipolar and mental illness. It worked if you took medicine for a year. Bipolar is curable if you take medicine and trust again. The people in your life, they of the mental health institute took protocol off with a wave. It came back if you went against the president in any way verbal or assassin. It came back quick. It was a computer that got into the nervous system and convinced you that your breathing would stop. Heart failure a pretense of voodoo and witchcraft. It caught you by surprise only if you served a God of love not hate or convince you that your wife was cheating, that your ugly brother was competing that the good looking one loved his wife more than you. The president loved seeing results through hospitalization for being rude. It was morbid and fruitful that the president goes even only in his mind. Programmers came up with it. The president turned it off for treatment only because they were sick.

Treatments good if you treat well. Richard Tye stated averting his eyes. The patients were nurses. You have to swallow medicine and process hateful thoughts out. The news said that Joker was a big fat zoo animal. Joker had potential of killing someone and playing them for as long as he wanted, forty years or until eighty. He was one trillion years old and took over time and two times and recreated the planet.

Gotham came and went far beyond times spectrum. Joker come in through Saddam and Gomorrah. The people went to the devil in Saddam and Gomorrah. Upon doing so the police picked up anything good. The military was ineffective, venomous snakes and spiders took over the population, one trillion one billion times. The year was the future of past time. People like parades. Gotham had ten major cities. They knew of the Joker none. He was very sneak. There were no humans that he did not or could not dictate, manipulate or control. He was an alpha meaning AAA species of spiders that rules people. Like chocolate cake in the refrigerator on wax paper. He consumed humans one hundred percent. The same as chocolate cake being eaten. He never killed babies. The spider kingdom with an active mind never killed infants, babies, or kids because they were young and could grow up strong and be manipulated and used for a food supply later. It was unbelievable the existence of these devils of death. Joker had the capacity to kill one trillion people. The police created no problems for Joker or Al Capone. They were the only ones with the exception of Jed Clampit that killed police officers and won. The police were out arrest.

Steve received word that Indiana Jones thrived and was alive. Indy or Theodore Roosevelt was from Gotham. Of course we of not Indiana Jones from an Indiana theme park, let's call ourselves dug out. I don't know the head of the committee said, it sounds like a military term in it's in. Maybe. The dairy farmers sent a bunch of dummy cows to Africa I don't know if it's old dairy or not. If so they had better put them out to pasture. Kids in America will want those cows that produced a milk for cookies and peanut butter sandwiches our there mulching sweet pasture until they die. The cows were millions and Joker intercepted them because he ate them to sustain. I was Steve Black. Gotham was trillions of years past this location was space docks prepared for space odyssey. Joker came and went. All there was stillness. The Jokers existence was none. He was a black widow tarantula that ruled time. He died of lack of oxidation. He was black and tarantula. I would not be afraid of him. Steve wore a suite. All you would have to do is spray him. He dropped a suite and a black spider fell with an orange spot. There, the spider was Sebastian Bach. He was recreated one trillion years later. He was tarantulas as much as the Joker in many ways. The Joker wasn't around for trillions of years. Joker showed signs none. There was no reason to he was political accurate and everything he did and knew how to behave in situations. He was one hundred percent accurate and everything he did and knew the way in and out. He was the biggest to promote crime and get by with it.

The computer world opened up for some Stetson opened for entrance and exit. He opened movies that came out and went and got in through his detective agency. That means that accessibility of special effects was hits. Stetsons programmer creates an ego that went into his nervous system and offered environment by computer. An environment, it was pleasant. She placed the environment in Stetson's memories and tried to burn off bad memories with good programmability. It chased away bad memories and warmed the memories in your mind. The ego mean high enthusiasm. Stetson's programmer picked up his grades and education from school and traced memories to equal performance into the military. The ego was a magnificent device that burnt off control through any mind manipulation. If it existed your areas and thoughts were clearer and more sharply defined. If your plan and design of life was good it helped in certainty the grades from school helped with scope and utilized your output in a rational way. The ego would bring in the precise environment of school memories of occurrences and military experiences. It was a charge that chased away negativity and doubt and brought good environment for example popcorn popped when it wasn't anywhere around. Judd Nelson's output in the Breakfast Club bought packages of a high school student that stayed in for a day or the seventies/eighties martial artist packages bought kershak and his confidence. You knew that you did not have the martial arts experience or JR Erving there were ten actors that portrayed the manipulator of oil, one being the 1980 Don Johnson of Miami Vice who had output that was high or a high ego. The ego was a computer that was kept synched in your main computer and activated upon wake to winding down at bed time and went into a dream stage. It worked on graphics to charge you to invigorate you during the day and take you through the day. Music had song and environment if you liked it the ego helped.

"Hi, Barbara Roberts is my name. I need your help." She was very pretty and built well. Her makeup was flawless, her clothing fit well. Her cologne was good. "Do not use me in any capacity. I will pay well." Stetson smiled. "I'm Stetson a Detective Agency. We are not set on prices. The state knows the prices. I will give it to you straight. I'm legal by the United States State Department." Stetson smiled. "I am very good at what I do and the final report will be conclusive." Barbara smiled. She was at ease. Her education was high. Her husband was in oil, he died. She hated it. Barbara liked him a lot, and wished that she had kids by him. "What can I do for you?" Stetson asked. "I have three houses, one is in Florida. I had a book club or meetings we choose books and read and discussed them. We brewed hot tea or iced or apple cider and had banana bread. It kept your mind clicking and connecting. We went out and ate fine dining and all friends tried connecting me with males to date. I really didn't want to meet anyone. I kept my agenda and schedule full. I played a clown at a book club meeting. No one knew who I was. It was a surprise. What are you writing down?" She asked. Stetson smiled. "Just main ideas so I can help you in those areas by knowing these areas." "This situation really gets adrenaline of fear pumping through my whole self." Stetson smiled his office was spotless. "Please continue." He smiled. "I was at a book meeting where we spoke of current books. I decided to go over to a friend's house with fudge and lollipops even apple cider. Her son Andy was celebrating his birthday. I changed into a neutral clown you could not tell if I was male or female." Barbara was very pretty. Her education was highly sophisticated usually if shown in sales of business there was usually an output or a reason to meet. In demonstration events could be costly to promote yourself as rich, you could sell product and take orders, self-help emotions feelings. Recovery oriented was usually processed well through the state approval. These organizations sold books to help process your life. Well from recover from alcoholism, drug addiction, sexual output considered healthy. People in alcoholic families, drug recovery etc. The state psychiatry could diagnose you through counseling and on output of organizations, church service was a Free State organization whether condemning or not your life should be more moralistic with an output of what is good or bad for you. Hence life should be with more longevity these organizations of the state are self-assured good if you understand titled. In psychiatry if diagnosed and the doctor and counselor sends you then hopefully you can process your emotions and feelings. Better if you can understand in current language what is being said. The same for church service and any other state service the counselor in the treatment has to have a certificate of state. The minister has to have one. They work for the state and are paid for and educated by the state. If you have work detail you have to keep your occupation up whether a counselor sends you to a state doctor paid for by the state or location that accepts medical insurance. If after treatment a relapse occurs down the road a relapse back into thinking bought you into a counselor or a use of drugs all is state and listed under mental illness. That keeps some away also lockdown ward some can find very intimidating. However you get out in the...

Exxon was established early. Exxon was a penitentiary that was designed to keep prisoners in. The wardens stayed a life time and retired and stated in level B, Basement they meet and ate at all the executives. It was a state facility that fed the same as school lunches, medical was also provided. The guards were taught nobody ever escaped without complete sentence upon flying out of Exxon penitentiary. The coordinators was lost in the computer. The staff couldn't find their way out. The electricity was off, the phone system off too.

Joker shook under a blanket, he was tough. His stint with crime was supposed to be over being incarcerated if you hired and business wanted legal one hundred percent, they didn't want to be stolen from or robbed. However, being sentenced and sent to jail and the penitentiary your name was called the city police and the state police knew your name, you would not hire them because they were unsuccessful in crime because they were caught. Jokey was different; he behaved criminally with the guard. Whether he had military experience or learned to fight off the street he was criminal against a guard that was eaten by rodents that possessed venom. He made a mistake on his transport out.

Saddam and Gomorra entered the facility with two million venomous animals. The devils from zoos and the wild of Saddam and Gomorra had the future in computers to some who entered the complex. Even take on humans. Joker shook he had a high resistance to poison and venom. The rats gave nutrients of twenty percent. The rattle snakes were big, unbelievable in size. Havana had really large venomous spiders and snakes. They were bandits and devil unbelievable. In scary venom gave the snakes an air meant of evil, the rattle snakes were mean looking. They took on their last victim and looked like them.

The cell door opened the rattle snake looked like the warden. He opened Joker's cell and let him go. Joker looked up, he needed a shave. His eyes were control, like Al Capone may have been, Jim Jones, or Charles Manson if he were a great leader. He was shut down on his first crime and it was unexplained during a time of sex, drugs, rock and roll, and the protest of the war. Joker had a look in his eyes of a big crime leader. Joker was taken to the warden's office. Joker had a look in his eyes of a big crime leader. Joker was taken to the warden's office. The warden sat down, "Do you have a hook up to our central computers?" "Yes", the warden said. "May I?" Joker asked. "Yes." Joker was behind a computer screen, he typed in to the computer re-enter-organization. The screens lit up the Joker's organization. The list was two million venomous animals from Saddam and Gomorra. The computer lit up two rodents' deceased recreate. The computer lit up upon consuming the rats, you will have strange appetite. Your system overcame well. Joker entered a remake of the penitentiary. The penitentiary was remake. The whole pen was the same. The guard was back. Joker took it down on remake 1000 level. Joker entered access to Gotham Illinois to Los Angeles. He could do a remake of any location as the leader of Saddam and Gomorra because the computers were expensive. His tribe came after him one hundred percent of the time when the Joker was in trouble.

Harry Callahan was told to arrest someone his captain. His plaques read: Lieutenant Harry Callahan Commissioned F.B.I. Joker sat behind his desk at the bottom it said: Commissioned by Joker. Joker looked like an ant that was as big as your head. The captain said, "Who are you?" The Joker went out to eat real meat probably rodent. Joker looked like a black ant. His last victim, the waitress said, "What are you?" She smiled, "Are you human? Maybe we should get Harry Callahan to look at you." What he did wrong was he didn't say what I look like. Instead he ran out. He looked like an ant for two weeks. He thought that he looked like himself. Harry said something about his aunt talking about Joker. His aunt said, "I want Joker dead and everything of his dead." The Joker was really progressed at crime to kill. Harry's aunt as a cousin to crime, Harry was talking about the Joker looking like an ant. He did not know that his aunt would be involved. Her dog bit him after contending so he looked like the dog.

Harry Callahan, the newly acclaimed F.B.I was out. "The captain said that I must arrest someone who do you suggest?" He said. Harry was quick with law enforcement he was trained for it. His house was a flat. It had two rooms, a basement, kitchen and bathroom. It was medium sized. Harry arrested a jaywalker for smarting off and took him before the captain for prosecution. He apologized and the captain let him pay a fine and said go. "Harry Callahan F.B.I. prosecuted you; you can go back and tell your friends that you were arrested by Harry Callahan." The office was Lieutenant Harry Callahan; Joker looked like a red ant. He ate a normal sized ant after the rats. Joker took on his last victim. He thought that he looked like Joker, he went out and for two weeks people laughed at him. Finally he looked in the mirror and returned to normal. He wanted Harry out only if he went against him.

The next day Harry Callahan was a licensed F.B.I. agent with a badge. Two weeks later "Hi, I am Sidd. Harry is a sissy that likes to be tied up, let's get together and homosexualize him in embarrassing ways for a male." The leader Kate laughed. There were seven of them. They walked into the bank a .38 in their hand. "Okay, your money." He proclaimed. "We want Dirty Harry out of commission, he's a sissy." Harry waived, he had just made a withdrawal. Joker watched from behind, he knew what they did wrong. He had no involvement but to laugh. Harry waived three times, he looked male. After the robbery he walked out, he was wearing a brown suite with a tie. He liked brown. "Okay, why?" He asked male was for him for a moment any way. "Because, you're a kinky swine that likes to be tied up," the leader proclaimed. "I'm not bad yet you are. You are under arrest." The reason he spoke that was Harry was scared and couldn't articulate his words well. "Okay you're under arrest," Harry said for the second time "Go for your guns or I'll kill you at point blank range." The men drew. Seven were killed at point blank range with a .44 Smith and Wesson, the most powerful handgun. It went clear through your head. Nobody ever used one because it boomed instead of cracked. Seven people were dead. Afterwards they called him Dirty Harry, because he killed instead of arresting.

Dirty Harry Callahan was exempt in a minute. "I did not mean to kill them, please forgive me. You can have my badge." Harry stated. Stetson was up and about he met a new girlfriend He still was not over his wife that was killed by the Cubans. It was amazing that the United States military would hold the country their own through a president; President Byers on trade. The military took hostage the F.B.I. for minutes, Cuba for years until one million was distributed. Stetson's wife was very important. Cuba was brutal. He loved her very much. President Byers stopped the process of warfare against the president's own country. It showed up none. Stetson hurt deep into his heart and soul. It had been while. She was pretty, her build was ace. He liked her. Her name was Tina Marcum. She was a secretary for a law firm. They spoke well, intimate and like each other His detective careers was enough to support him. Timmy dropped by occasionally, he went places with. She was engaged to Mark Withim, a business executive. Stetson was happy. He bought a nice wedding present and went to the wedding. He was happy.

Stetson had a computer that he had permission to hook up to a military computer. All wars were listed with the names of Generals and leaders. When a detective was needed was when your mind was computer boggled on a situation and your output of your profession, you're not told. The reason you lost in the area, some wanted relationships resolved if told a private detective. It broke a code of silence and the organization knew that you were being reported in to someone involved with someone in your lie to uncover answers a snoop that reported in. Stetson was a pro, he could develop a team to restore or provide information. Restore cost more. Stetson received credential in business reports. He had computer programs that got him in and out of locations. He was a spirt fire.

England did well enough with Egypt if they would have kept Egyptian clothing eventually they would have paid a lot of money. Egypt knew how to collect. They would send someone intimidating with a gun as an over take. Egypt was old and very clever; no one knew that original race was Cuban in America and throughout the Middle East. The Egyptians spoke fluently and lived well through time and picked up on hundred percent. On Egypt, Harry Callahan would say, "I don't know much about them, just what they taught me in school. They are foreign and in the Middle East, so I am not concerned about them. If they come to the country legal I will be polite. If the state department wants them out I'd get them out."

Her name was Lisa Cole. She was built AAA. Harry was fond of her. He called her baby and Lassie. He cuddled with her seldom. "Did you tell them that I like to be tied down angel?" Harry asked. "Yes, because you do, you're not kinky about it." "I'm not kinky, kinky means that you like spankings, being whipped and abused by guys. They call them sissy's" "You're not kinky, I know the female organization, that it was part of the package to fix you up with pretty women."

Two days later the Joker held handcuffs up. "Hey Harry do you want these? You may want a spanking next." Joker ran off. He knew that kinky sex was a ruin because guys didn't like that form of being over taken. The enemy and other guys thought that if a women could whip them in bed they could. Women were equal in smarts. Their output was according to training. Guys may or may not view a flower the same and some women claimed on home making yet the education was the same. Harry liked women well. Joker met with the organization that attempted the robbery. He was red, and looked like an ant. You not Harry Callahan has a female organization that backs him with women. You can take advantage of him if you can go through them. Joker left an umbrella he thought that he looked like himself. He looked like an ant. The organization was a hunters club. They were mean with weapons. The leader Hence Brodwell spoke to their leader Mrs. Thomas and asked Dirty Harry to record. "Well Mrs. Thomas told he like to be tied down and coos like a mocking bird when perturbed." "Get the weapons ready that mans a sissy." They went in with weapons upon Harry making a withdraw.

Joker was a crack with crime. He got by with it because he was quick with get always. Stetson invested money in movie packages for example, Steven Spielberg realizing Jurassic park and he had three to five released and probably one thousand movies. Stetson bought packages for the computer not commercial. He turned the packages over to his programmer and she utilized them for him. He bought on thousand movies of Indian Jones. Legally he was told to look out for any Egyptians because they collected on anything Egypt. The movie packages improved his output at home and work. Upon running them through and ordering computer stores that promoted Stetson and got him in and out of situations. He was keen and had a stoic mind.

Harry ran in did what he wanted to. He was F.B.I. and hired. He knew if he was fired he was very high in output. He killed only during crime and gun play. Joker was clever in knowing how to maneuver around him. He arrested quick, prosecuted quick and sent them to the penitentiary quick. His life was one hundred percent because he knew how to behave in public. At one point of Dirty Harry's life he was asked if he wanted to be in the movies, he signed and said, "Masculine only occasionally." The fiction was written into the movies and it played in districts differently. Good morning the law is the law, you oblige, I oblige. How old are you. Thirty eight years old. The year was 1972.

The police were high in output. Workmanship was high. "Hi how are you. The spider king is at bay. We have only two Sebastian back and Siddy Earl." "I'm not a spider," Siddy said, "I'm not a spider my name is Tim Albright." The speaker had kind of sandy brown hair. He was the police commissioner. His jeans were Lee. He was thirty four years old. He spoke for one hour and a half on local events of Los Angeles.

A Sherriff named Buford from Tennessee arrested two blacks and hung them because they were black. He smiled; they put their name on the Albany Court House dead, dead, dead. The Albany Court House laughed and said they went that way to continue to see their shadows black run running to hell. The congregation laughed. Ten blacks went out the door. If they're that prejudice we want to leave. The blacks were educated college. Can we get credit, they were prejudice against me. The secretary Heidi said "No, you have to settle it with the leader sir." She said to the commissioner. "Can they get their money back? The said you were prejudice." The commissioner looked at them. He was a good looking guy to; the blacks ugly because he wanted to take rights from them. The commissioner smiled. He liked the blacks. "I like you, you can stay." Then he went on. They slipped out the back door. The whole congregation was robbed. The whole congregation was ignorant on who robbed them. The commissioner knew who it was. He lost two stereos and one hundred dollars. It was equivalent to one thousand today. They had no idea why they robbed them. It was because they tried taking self-esteem from them as blacks and their rights to zero.

The two blacks were in San Diego, they were no arrested in Tennessee because they were legal. They saw Buford once. He said, "Don't let the door hit you where the good Lord split you. You're black go by sun down." "Yes, Mr. Pulser Buford Pulser." We left two days later. We were legal going in and leaving. They signed in the government on black issues. They won't use you unless you sign. They say the sign and smiled. We are less than to them, more to ourselves. "The sign said leave or we will split you with an axe. Buford hated you, we do too." Upon seeing it the blacks smiled. The was us; we live in a prejudice world. Pay us those people were southern and prejudice against a race from the United States. The blacks were college educated and smiled, we signed. Their life was one hundred percent. They went whites way none, they robbed none. Each had ten kids, the kids lived well.

Buford Pulser has it made. He speaks of black and got by with it. Sheriff Montgomery Pride from Birmingham Alabama spoke well only of Buford Pulser. He's a law man and a half. Montgomery arrested two blacks that day for loitering. He fed them chocolate cake and stated, "You are illegal, and you have a ticket to court. Bubba tell them that the United States is full of blacks when they congregate together. Their septic goes bad because one of the blacks didn't pay for septic. He bought drugs. Education is that way; get a ticket that you went to school. Tell them Montgomery sent you and you black and need to be educated. They were educated college quick. Their education was high school. Sheriff Montgomery was good to blacks because he offered discipline in the state department to site them. Sheriff Montgomery was good to the blacks, great if you know that he prosecuted them well while Sheriff Buford Pulser killed them with a gun and took their bodies out because he hated blacks.

Buford Pulser from Jamestown Tennessee started a black boot hill because he hated blacks. He age was twenty three. Buford Pulser was a sheriff because he was prudent at crime. He lost fights seldom. Once a six foot black man hit him with a chair breaking his nose. His name Steve Lawrence stated, "I'm sorry I didn't mean to hit him." The bartender Linda Evans said, "I'm sorry." She smiled, "No, woman rights issues here." That meant women disrespected on restroom breaks. Buford nose is broke said, "Women's rights are passed in Washington." Buford output was twenty eight when he walked in he ordered a martini. Steve Lawrence shook his hand. He was black. He said, "My names Buford Pulser." He towered six feet and was one hundred percent on output because he worked out all the time, his output was one hundred. "I'm Buford Pulser; I'm going to law school to become a copy." Buford said.

Steve shook his hand. Buford stated, "I don't need any doubles." Steve was moving the bar chair when it hit Buford it was a mistake. The next day at Steve's house was sold and he was placed in the jail for thirty days. They only do that when you're black and violent against whites. Upon going to court, Judge Tomas said guilty or innocent. "Of what I did nothing." Steve Lawrence was college educated. The only way he showed it was he could read and write.

"You hit Buford Pulser with a chair." The judge stated. The judge resided in Jamestown Tennessee. "I like Buford Pulser." Steve was released. Buford had tape on his nose. He shook Steve's hand, "There's no animosity?" Buford asked. "None sir, did you have me arrested?" Steve asked. "No." Buford responded, "It was housing, the said your house was sloppy. Steve's house was spotless. It was not me." Buford stated. The black man believed him. The black man Steve was prosecuted twenty two times because Buford said give him the treatment. The state police of Tennessee came in on Steve Lawrence once a day. Two other issues were blacks that hit Buford on using racial terms, twice. His nose was broken the second time his jaw. They were prosecuted, Buford was wrong in both situations. The blacks output was high in output. Buford was twenty eight percent after the blacks were zero. They were none in other fights. Buford took being sheriff and was sheriff for twenty eight years, because he was good at prosecution. When he was thirty eight he signed off for real life in the movies. He was in Walking Tall. The first actor favored him in looks. His output was one hundred percent.

Alabama Birmingham 1972 Sheriff Montgomery Pride had two hundred deputies. There were three divisions of sheriff's departments in Birmingham. They were at crime, they won one hundred percent. When illegals were turned in Montgomery Pride was an excellent sheriff. He was sheriff for twelve years reelected. He was respected because he was portly and had high output as a sheriff. At twenty three he signed to be in the movies. He said, "Shave some weight off." The series that portrayed his life was: In the Heat of the Night, starring Carol O'Conner. Stetson bought and the programmer utilized he was quick at getting in and out.

The house was extra nice, electric and water was owed monthly. "You are recreating." The company was owned by the state. You will be taken care of by the company legalized. Workmanship of eight hours and you will be paid. Jesse Adams woke up. The environment was stimulating. He though well of coffee. He drank. He was uplifted. He drank the coffee and utilized or tried to organize his thoughts. He had outlets here for work and promise he felt well. He would apply for work and try to have output that was high.

The location was complete country with automobiles, hospitals, grocery stores, and a complete state. Workmanship would be high, the holidays respected. It was placed together by the state for recreation of people from the United States legal by God and state. The location had was moral, the population was high trillions the out of this state. Recreation was high. The location was legal. An older man sat at a fast food restaurant near the kid section. The location had slides and arcades that went through mazes kind of like a hamster world. That was colorful. A little girl trotted over, "Is that fun?" The older man named Mike asked. Cathy was five. She raised her hands above her head. The reason she didn't know what he was talking about. He was just asking if the kids slide was as fund as it looked . He thought of a metropolitan areas he was at one. He felt therapeutic almost a dream. The environment was good. He looked across the street and swings and monkey bars. The environment was almost ba ba boom. A zoo animal lightly in the environment. It was pleasant. Mike just wore up. He was in treatment recovering from alcoholism. His IQ was high. The kids played on the swings and titter totters and the environment was good.

Years later the little girl said, "Haven't you tried that yet?" Brenda the girl's mother asked Mile the older man. Mike smiled, "No, no I'm much too old for it." "Let's go", Brenda said with a smile. "She went on the hamster ride in the kid section and so did Mike. They both sat on the floor and spoke. He liked it. The mother liked it partaking in the ride was fun. He felt better because he connected with someone. Jesse works up well in a forever world that was for him. The manufacturing company of this eternity was not against God or the state. Jesse was recreated and distributed food a place to stay and to be incorporated in the job related world. Jesse's record was known by the state department. He was protected by the state department if illegal he would be cited and fined by the state. Education was available the same. The school systems in the United States. Computers of eternity were A to Z, turned into the United States. State department money was legalized through the United States. Eternity has treatment and churches and law departments etc., and a united government seal legal. The movies went from G to XXX entertainment.

Chicago Illinois. "Hi young man do you have the money for the government wave?" Harry waved sideways and it goes away and comes back none. Stage goes off. IN your mind no protocol or activist and turns that cause you to see devils in the night?" Harry Callahan said. "Are you prejudicing against blacks?" Sanders were ten. "No I don't hate your skin color only that your legal or not." Dirty Harry said. "Maybe we should let the Joker settle this. He's mean real mean." Sanders said. Harry was back in the his office in one minute. The Joker's rules were symbolic around Harry's office. He looked like a red ant because that was what he last consumed. He scurried away unseen.

Harry looked at his calendar and went to a business meeting. He left there was two arrests for marijuana a black kid ten and a jay walker. Harry called the uniformed police. Harry saw his girlfriend, "Kinky not?" He inquired. She was very pretty and built AAA. "Rope burns," she said. "I had to do that or no woman would be sent by your agency." Your clear and you behaved well." She smiled and blew him a kiss. Harry was aggressive at law enforcement. He won because he was prudent with weapons. She was a secretary and showed up for work at six a.m. "Harry's good for me, he wasn't kinky. I wish he would take the Joker out and kill him." The door to her office was shut. She was killed. The other secretary didn't even see her body taken out. Harry had no idea that Joker killed her. She called and broke up was all that Harry Callahan knew. The women's organization presented Dirty Harry with a new date two weeks later. He didn't even suspect anything was wrong. Joker left no sign. Dirty Harry's gun was two million males on hold up.

At the start of his career as an F.B.I. in Gotham, Harry Callahan met with a woman's organization on dating. Harry wore a brown suite, a black tie. He loved brown suites because his eyes were brown. His race was Italian. "What do I need to do to keep a woman? Just date them and let them tie you up once and speak only that you complied?" "Isn't that kinky?" Harry had two guns, two smith and Wesson, forty four. The woman knew that and respected it. "Just let the Joker handle them if they get out of line." "I need a new representative." Harry stated. She mentioned illegal like it was a consequence for behavior. Harry stated, "In an officer of the law and try to remain legal. Do disrespect to you Harry was backed with a smile." "Sorry I go." She said.

A new representative presented herself. She was AAA in build. The last representative went to her office the Joker went in. "Mrs. Flannigan." He corrected. "Why would I be a representative for bad behavior? You can go after them only if they go against Harry. We will keep them coming. Harry is a state copy with weapons, charm and charisma. His IQ is high. I want him alive not dead. The Joker can have them when he's done with them." She was very pretty. "Ok I am." He ran out. Larry smiled. "Just hold up your hand and state sex modified none." She was extra fine in build and pretty. "Boy your eyes are brown and you're brilliant." Larry smiled. "You're in time just turn them over to the Joker. When you're finished." Harry smiled. "Bye." "You're in for a life time of dates because you're extravagant."

Harry dated Sona Barr. He went out with her five hundred times. Upon going out to eat people spoke to him none because he was good with guns. His last girlfriend died by the Joker. The thing that surprised be was Harry's being tied down. They liked Dirty Harry F.B.I. In details that he was like a state copy. His smith and Wesson back that Dirty Harry was respected highly because he was deadly with guns. He gave the air that he wasn't afraid of the Joker and his killings he was the dates respect for Dirty Harry Callahan. He was unbelievably high. He was F.B.I. and wore suits that fit this and had an air of charm. One time they were disappointed and wanted to die because he broke up with them. Harry signed for the movies, Clint Eastwood starred in Dirty Harry and Raw Hide was original and other westerns on into The Outlaw of Josey Wells, whether taken from Dirty Harry or the reenactment of the 1800 confederate army war. The war explains weaponry and overtakes of ranches during the 1800's Clint Eastwood had A to Z a lot of movies into Any Which Way but Loose to Bronco Billy, Dirty Harry was an aspect of his career.

Dirty Harry made a withdrawal. Earlier at 6:15 a.m. the banks appeared in Gotham Illinois. "Give Harry some money at least one hundred, the sissy likes to be tied up." The banker said he was perturbed because his daughter was killed by the Joker and Harry laughed instead of crying. Joker slithered in he looked like a rat because his men turned by eating the food. "What's with that rat?" He thought that he looked like himself. He looked like a rat. He squeaked instead of vocals. "Get the gun and kill the rat." Joker went out. "Why does Dirty Harry kill women by stating he likes to be tied up?" The banker Carl stated. "I want him dead." He took a pistol out, "I want him dead." Dirt Harry woke up at 8:00. He behaved wrongfully once under whips and chains and owned up to sex people stated at a town meeting. He was exempt. He was angry when people ask his name. He said Dirty Harry Callahan they said go. He went. They weren't after him except he killed them in seconds.

The banker Carl had a gun and a one hundred dollar bill; he won one hundred percent of the money back from Gotham Illinois. Joker processed it back, his money was good. "Dirty Harry killed my baby and I want him dead. Joker entered the conversation what he dispensed was a gun and one million currency. He wanted Harry Callahan provoked only not killed, he put the gun to his head and fired because he was F.B.I. "How much money do you have Harry?" "One million dollars." Harry smiled. "Pay me." You bet guns were presented. Harry looked at them, "What's this about?" "You're a sissy that likes to be tied up." "Hold it I have a gun." Harry was nervous. It showed none. "Okay" The banker helf his hand out and Harry reached for his gun. "Fine was the order they fired on." Harry caught two bullets one in the hip one in the eye. It paralyzed him for one day.

At the hospital the nurse asked if he was kinky. Harry wined and said no was the truth. He looked a chase who was chase because she wore female well and was very good looking. He liked her. "Did you say kinky?" He asked. "No," she lied. She was suggestive of sex every time she spoke. She stated two days later Harry like to be tied up. He was hope recuperating his eye was healed. Modern medicine was expensive. "If you say kinky I will break up with you." Women's output in the secretary's woman club was high in secretary. They were AA down to expensive lingerie. Men wore bikini underwear. Boxers and white and placed things on looks highly. Women had output training on the job and output. Blacks were the same, Hispanics, Mexicans etc. If the woman of Harry's club wanted to be brilliant at sex they could. Their style of dress was up to them and the dress code of their company. Number three was gone out of Harry's death pool. He card because she was brilliant at sex. His company of F.B.I. and through life without speaking of it. Dirty Harry signed up for women that were AAA providers to a sex addict of male that gained weapons of a high caliber. They knew that he would kill them upon sex announcement. Harry healed from his wounds one hundred percent in three years. He limped and his eyes swelled up.

The three men were dead. The banker and the gunman died when Harry revealed the gun and fired Harry's not after with two bullets in him. The ten died, Joker was on the wall, a rodent. Saddam and Gomorrah was an interesting for venom. Dirty Harry met a woman under distress called Anderson, outside the secretary pool or death pool with secretaries with too much lingerie, too much sex appeal and a lot of pretty's. Harry was like a female black widow tarantula, though male that mated and killed. It showed up seldom upon dying. An 89 Harry had two sons, Stetson and Steve and was a school teacher. He left behind a trail of dead bodies. He learned to mate to kill. Through the Joker killing women upon being tied down his sexual was straight. He killed under bank robbery only when they called him a sissy that mean the woman spoke of his being tied down, he exaggerated anything that lead to a ruin sexual hence forth winning in the death pool. Before ruin in his department of F.B.I. and the secretary's. The woman found him enticing as a straight Italian and very control or rated. He solved every case one hundred percent. His sons were trained by him on hundred percent in weaponry. Harry's dirty ways were taught without his conscious thought by his upbringing by criminal law. He had a malicious mid for crime and prevention.

Sex was in devils sometimes outlet was different or the same with romance or none. There was XXX clubs that varied masculine or pretty outlet and qualifying was the individual. There were male dancers, guys didn't seem to like them or incorporate them in the business world modifying sex was an organization of AAA secretaries that would ruin or not in only in their secretary pool people. Male and female married, single, cheated on family oriented behaved usually well in the country. Bosses usually incorporated workmanship and formally kept sexual content away from kids usually. Some locations had extra in other locations and modified sexual content out during a work day for workmanship and sought dates and wives at home during the weekend.

The speaking of religion was rare yet some wars were taught under religious leaders of God of Satan. Usually people went to church and knew nothing about how to serve Satan. Sin maybe ways were wars the output was trainings, freezer units may take an army through time. The units states somehow with a future from at least 1900 protocol of the president processing money to the tax department. Somehow a unit was created that could freeze a human at their age until they were taken out of unit's the same age hours, days, monthly years. When the units were turned off and they came out they were the same age. The units showed through time invented none. They spoke of people dying of disease and being frozen until there was a cure. These froze alive and they came out alive. So far they hadn't been known to be invented. Frozen was against people, they were frozen upon a court marshaling event. On the United States military finding them guilty of speaking while a hostage. The president was over the conspiracy. The F.B.I. would place the person the rest of his life and he would be frozen. It was a form of death. People believed that the black market was responsible. It was the president. The F.B.I. played the United States citizens there was even an electric service. These processes were older yet very future and people spoke of the situation none for fear of being hostage. American's believed that they were the only ones that was hostage. Only one individual self in a cubicle one hundred percent of the United States went under once the replacement was F.B.I. Another time Cuba, another Confederate Army under Clampit. The Confederacy was as capable of death and anything listed end of time or Satan. The Bible listed the Garden of Eden as the starting point. We were taught that the United States was young. The Middle East old and traditional and the starting point the planet Earth. Yet it seemed that confederate army gave a location of death or life and brought in a population recreated in the devil himself.

The location of confederacy was as traditional as the south. Jed's going out on tax invasion made him very spiteful very evil, A to Z. The confederacy had one trillion devils, one billion times recreated from Hell. Sports centralized America one hundred percent. It was a fun rivalry. If you centralized a country like a sporting event you had some of the basketball commercials said a lot of hype. Metropolitan schools played high school, college, and pro. Sometimes the commercials actions were high in basketball and the state which the proceeds went sold more in areas promoted. The game was central centralized America. If spoken well of a sparkling water from for example the rain forest, would be plentiful if fresh water were commercialized or specialized brew of coffee. If that was made from water purified from Colorado to bring out a special roast of Caribbean coffee lives. Maybe you thought of the commercials of specialized bottle water for all occasions. One for example brought out orange in kool aid for Halloween. Basketball promotions went up on commercialized because it seemed to bring the quality out and you expected to see excitement, rivalry was fun. If you liked to speak well of your team while others were critical, commercials sold cleaners that were almost drinkable or dish detergent. It was the same for sports. If you were introduced well you knew how to appreciate from slogans on sports jackets that proceeds went into the state. The state received a big pay from sporting events. If sports afforded entertainment for you and that's what it was and you felt that you received your money's worth. It was then worth it.

They loved sporting events anytime throughout time. You saw it in jerseys, tee shirts, banners, stickers, etc. Movies were a lot of fun from a full day of work to school series that came on, movies on cable, popcorn, cokes, and video people likes to be entertained. Is showed in sales, the classic books were suggested in school were Sherlock Holmes etc. The classic movies from movies with no sound to black and white. Education gave an appreciation for the value of the state; Okayed and dispensed by the state department for safety etc. Entertainment, entertained only. You could see if the 1800's were introduced to cable TV or if you received a show time package with movies from the cinema brought right into your home packaged with un popped popcorn with specialized yellow cooking oil. The expense was you were detached and entertained. Other forms of entertainment were looking at the window at snowfall or rain and it was free. If provoked into thought by entertainment you thought something through if it became education then it had output. In the state department to be utilized for state education the same state the provided has patronization.

Steve Thomas was one son of Dirt Harry, Stetson was another. He raised his sons to know how to use guns and when to use them. Harry met their mom outside the secretary pool. The two sons were raised mostly by their mom. The confederacy was trillions of southerners that picked up anything of Satan. In any country and promoted against the country. It was difficult when religions were modified in because the leaders did not have a mailing address. Stetson solved cases, and was paid and liked his profession. He and his brother Steve Thomas met rarely. The New York school teacher went to his brother's wife's funeral. They got along well. They were both Dirty Harry Callahan's sons. Their last names were different; both were literal in their own way.

Egypt came and went. It dropped down deep into the Atlantis sun of fiction and blue ocean. What traces of mummification was there and what proof of the resurrection of pharaohs do we have. Steve Thomas was Dirty Harry's son. He slapped his forehead. I was raised enough in America to know that you recall someone from living not dead. The fictional movie version of the Egyptian Pharaohs was horror films and zombies. That meant corpses had human for no disrespect for the dead or Halloween, that came and went. Your assignment fact or opinions does the mention of Cleopatra cheapen or make Egypt expensive.

The bell rang well disguise it tomorrow. Steve Thomas closed the history book. It was his last class of the day. Steve called in and reserved a table for himself and his wife. His dad Harry Callahan knew no better than to be illegal because he was raised around crime. He was a great cop with the exception that when he broke up with a woman Joker moved in for the kill. He minded none because they tried ruins; Harry Callahan was equal to a black widow tarantula that was male. His death pool of secretaries died of criminal law after he broke up. He didn't care because they tried to ruin him on being tied down and he killed off all resistance in males when they stated he was a sissy.

Steve Thomas and Stetson's mom was different. He met her differently. She conceived all of his kids after wearing down hours. He fell asleep she woke up pregnant. He paid one hundred percent of the woman. In Gotham he wanted to have his kid because he wanted to show Dirty Harry the male tarantula that he was good with guns, masculine and Italian. The cases he tried were prosecuted one hundred percent because he was deadly at finding out information. Joker lived through animal behaviors and freezer units. He was precious in output.